D1450412

Alice Atherton's
GRAND TOUR

ALSO BY LESLEY M. M. BLUME

*Cornelia and the Audacious Escapades
of the Somerset Sisters*

Julia and the Art of Practical Travel

*Modern Fairies, Dwarves, Goblins,
and Other Nasties*

The Rising Star of Rusty Nail

Tennyson

*The Wondrous Journals of
Dr. Wendell Wellington Wiggins*

Alice Atherton's

GRAND TOUR

LESLEY M. M. BLUME

ALFRED A. KNOPF
NEW YORK

THIS IS A BORZOI BOOK PUBLISHED BY ALFRED A. KNOPF

This is a work of fiction. All incidents and dialogue, and all characters with the exception of some well-known historical and public figures, are products of the author's imagination and are not to be construed as real. Where real-life historical or public figures appear, the situations, incidents, and dialogues concerning those persons are fictional and are not intended to depict actual events or to change the fictional nature of the work. In all other respects, any resemblance to persons living or dead is entirely coincidental.

Visit us on the Web! rhcbooks.com

Educators and librarians, for a variety of teaching tools, visit us at RHTeachersLibrarians.com

Library of Congress Cataloging-in-Publication Data is available upon request.
ISBN 978-0-553-53681-2 (trade) — ISBN 978-0-553-53682-9 (lib. bdg.) —
ISBN 978-0-553-53683-6 (ebook)

The text of this book is set in 12.5-point Thorndale AMT.
Interior design by Michelle Crowe

Printed in the United States of America
10 9 8 7 6 5 4 3 2 1
First Edition

Random House Children's Books supports the First Amendment and celebrates the right to read.

FOR OONA HELENE
ESSENTIAL CONSULTANT, MERCILESS CRITIC,
AND ADORED DAUGHTER

AND FOR LAURA DONNELLY
WITH FRIENDSHIP AND ADMIRATION

Author's Note

While many of the characters in *Alice Atherton's Grand Tour* are well-known historical figures, this book is a work of imagination, and in its pages, these people, their conversations, and their actions—as well as some dates of real-life events and architectural details of the settings—have been made up, changed slightly, or fictionalized.

If you want to learn more about the lives of these complicated creative figures, there are many biographies about each for you to explore. Please ask your librarian or bookseller to help you find them.

Contents

Chapter One

THE RIGHT CURE

NEW YORK CITY, 1927. ALICE ATHERTON LOOKED OUT the window at the park across the street from her house. A light, pretty snowfall was turning the park's bushes and benches into white-hided, slumbering animals. Dusk was falling too.

Alice would have given anything to be outside in that snow, but instead she was stuck inside, subjected to an endless geography lesson by her governess, Miss Pennyweather. Alice secretly called her Old Miss Pennyweather, even though the governess probably wasn't all that old. She just happened to be gray in both face and spirit, and could make any subject under the sun impossibly dull. Old Miss Pennyweather could probably rob a bank and all of the tellers would fall asleep from boredom during the holdup.

Today's grueling lesson was taking place in the parlor. A roaring fire in the fireplace made the room hot and dry. Alice's cheeks burned pink and her head swayed from drowsiness.

"Cairo is an exotic city full of elaborate lore and mythology," Old Miss Pennyweather droned on. "But in ancient times, Alexandria was the true cultural capital of Egypt."

Here she paused.

"Alice, please point to Alexandria on this map."

But Alice did not point to Alexandria on the map. In fact, Alice did not even hear Old Miss Pennyweather's instruction. This is because she had fallen into a deep, rather sweaty daydream. In her mind, Alice had left the parlor minutes earlier and was out rolling around, like a happy dog, in all of that snow across the street.

"Alice Atherton!" exclaimed Old Miss Pennyweather, dropping a book on the floor with a rude *bang*. "Wake up this instant."

Swooning, Alice opened her eyes and looked blearily at her governess.

"Alice, this is the third time I've had to chastise you this afternoon," Old Miss Pennyweather thundered. "This is most regrettable behavior. Are you unwell?"

"I don't know," Alice muttered. "I'm just sleepy."

Old Miss Pennyweather swept over to Alice and clapped her papery hand onto the child's forehead.

"You may indeed be a touch warm," she said. "Oh dear, oh dear—what if it's the influenza? I'm certain that it's lingering in this filthy city. Or mumps? Or— God help us—scarlet fever?"

Old Miss Pennyweather bustled Alice out of the parlor and up the stairs into her bedroom.

"Mrs. Millicent," she called, summoning the house-keeper. "Bring a bowl of cold water at once. Send for the doctor. And please tell Mr. Atherton that Miss Alice has taken ill."

Old Miss Pennyweather shoveled Alice into her bed. Soon a large bowl of cold water materialized, and by the time the doctor arrived a few minutes later, Old Miss Pennyweather—perhaps inspired by her lecture on Egypt—had practically made Alice look like a mummy, swaddled in bands of chilly, wet towels.

The doctor listened to Alice's chest with his stetho-scope. He peered into her ears, eyes, and throat.

"Oh dear, Doctor," fretted Old Miss Pennyweather. "Please tell me that it's not the same terrible fever that took this child's mother six months ago. This house simply can't have another tragedy."

The doctor began packing up his equipment into a

little leather bag. "I think, Miss Atherton, that you are going to live," he said to Alice kindly.

"You'll be relieved to learn that there isn't a blessed thing wrong with her," he told Old Miss Pennyweather as he stood up. He felt a bit grumpy with the governess, as he had left behind a delicious dinner of roast beef and gravy to rush to Alice's bedside. That dinner—which had been hot and jolly just half an hour earlier—was now likely sitting there back on his dining-room table, cold and congealed.

"Well, thank heavens," exclaimed Old Miss Pennyweather. Sensing the doctor's annoyance, she shifted to self-defense: "One can't be too careful in this day and age: germs lurk everywhere." She apologetically ushered the doctor out the bedroom door.

Left alone at last, Alice lay in bed and stared out the window. It was now dark outside—a lovely, deep, inky blue darkness—but Alice could still see the snow falling.

Alice's mother had loved winter. She had loved fur muffs and stocking caps and mittens and boots. She had loved sleigh rides and Christmas and snowy walks through the park. She had even loved eating snow, although it had appalled Alice's father when she did it.

"Time passes more slowly in winter—did you

know that?" she had once told Alice as they rode down Fifth Avenue in their horse-drawn carriage, snuggled together under a blanket.

"That's silly," said Alice, happily breathing in her mother's perfume. "Time goes at the same speed in every season."

"No, no—it's absolutely slower in winter," insisted her mother. "And that's why it's my favorite season, because it also means that you, Alice, are growing more slowly during those months. I get to have you as my little girl for just a bit longer."

Alice felt the reverberation of the heavy front door closing as the doctor was sent back to his supper. Then, a few moments later, she heard muffled voices coming from her father's study, which was on the floor below her room. Alice peeled off the clammy mummy rags, tiptoed to the stairwell, and eavesdropped.

Old Miss Pennyweather was holding a conference with Alice's father, Mr. Atherton.

"What did the doctor say about her condition?" Mr. Atherton asked the governess.

"That there is nothing physically wrong with her," replied Old Miss Pennyweather. "But there clearly *is* something wrong with her. She appears to be sleepwalking through the days. Nothing interests her at the moment. She barely eats. She has been like a different child since Mrs. Atherton passed on, sir. I know that she's grieving, but to have no interest in life at all anymore?"

The grandfather clock ticked in the downstairs foyer. It had been draped in a black velvet shroud since Alice's mother had died. Alice knew that her father was smoking his pipe and listening and thinking, and when he was pipe-smoking and listening and thinking, he could never be rushed to answer.

"This has indeed been an exceptionally difficult period for all of us, Miss Pennyweather," said Mr. Atherton at last. "And clearly none of us here have the solution for how to help Alice. Neither the doctor, nor I, nor you."

There was another moment of silence.

"Let me give the matter more thought," Mr. Atherton said eventually. "I believe that we need a creative solution, perhaps something even a bit unconventional."

Alice imagined Old Miss Pennyweather's response to this: she probably looked like she'd just tasted an especially sour lime. The mention of anything unconventional was repellent to her.

The governess retreated from the study and began to climb the stairs. Alice scuttled back into her room, dove into her bed, pulled up the covers to her chin, and squeezed her eyes shut. Her governess peeked in and, thinking that Alice had fallen asleep, left again in relief, closing the door behind her quietly.

Alice waited until she heard Old Miss Penny-weather's footsteps climb the stairs to her room on the top floor. She reached over to her bedside table and picked up a small gold brooch that had once belonged to her mother. The shape of a bunch of lilies of the valley, the brooch had flowers made of small pearls. Alice pinned it to the collar of her nightgown and tip-toed downstairs to her father's study. There she stood timidly in the doorway and gazed at him.

Mr. Atherton wore thick glasses. He was the president of a publishing company, and over the years, his eyes had grown tired from reading millions and millions of words. Bookshelves lined his study walls from floor to ceiling, and dozens of books stood in tall, crooked stacks all around the room.

"Hello, Papa," Alice said quietly.

Her father looked up from a manuscript that he was reading.

"Come in, little goose," he said.

Even though Alice was relatively tall for a ten-year-old, she climbed up onto her father's lap and nestled her head onto his shoulder. He touched the lilies-of-the-valley brooch on her collar, and gave her a gentle kiss on the top of her head.

"Are you feeling better?" Mr. Atherton said, smoothing down her hair. "Miss Pennyweather was in quite a state this evening."

"I was just tired," Alice told him.

"Why are you so tired?" her father asked her. "Aren't you sleeping well at night?"

"It's not that," she told him. "I'm just always sleepy right now. And not just when Miss Pennyweather is being boring in our lessons."

Mr. Atherton smiled. "Well, she does her best," he said. "Although I know that she's no substitute for your mother."

"No," Alice replied, and now she pressed her face against her father's chest so he couldn't see her crying.

Mr. Atherton smoothed Alice's hair until her breathing became calm and even again.

"Little goose, I know how difficult things have been since your mother died," he said a few minutes later. "I have been thinking tonight about how to help you. At first, I thought that keeping up your familiar routine here at home would be best. We'd already had so much change. But now I've come to the conclusion that the solution to your great unhappiness likely does not lie in this house. There is still too much sadness in it, and I think that you need lightness—and life."

Alice had no idea what he meant, but she tilted her face up and looked at him while he talked.

"I have just had a rather unusual idea," Mr. Atherton said. "But it would involve an adventure."

"Would you be coming along on the adventure too?" asked Alice.

"I wish I could," he told her. "I can't leave my work here in New York, and anyway, this journey is one that will be given to you by someone else."

"So the adventure is outside New York, then?" Alice pressed.

"Yes, but of course I would ask Miss Pennyweather to accompany you," replied Mr. Atherton. "It might seem at first like a big undertaking, but I feel certain that this adventure would be life-changing—and full of happy surprises. Do you think that you could be open to the idea?"

Alice was growing curious. "Where would I be going?" she asked her father.

"It's a secret—for now," he told her. "Do you trust me?"

Alice thought for a minute. She didn't like the idea

of being away from her father, but she did like the idea of happy surprises and lightness and life. Her mother had always said yes to adventures. So perhaps Alice should too. She nodded at her father.

"I'll put things in motion tomorrow," he told her. "Let's see what happens."

◦◦◦

EARLY THE NEXT MORNING, a messenger came to fetch a telegram written by Mr. Atherton to some mystery recipient. A day later, the messenger returned with a reply. More telegrams were carted in and out after that, and then, *finally,* about a week later, Mr. Atherton called Old Miss Pennyweather and Alice into his study.

"Miss Pennyweather," he said, "please have Mrs. Millicent arrange for our travel trunks to be taken out of storage as soon as possible."

"What for, sir?" said Old Miss Pennyweather, who generally did not care for traveling more than three or four city blocks in any direction. The idea of foreign foods, foreign beds, and foreign toilets filled her with foreboding.

"I'm delighted to report that you will soon be departing for France," Mr. Atherton answered. "To spend late spring and the whole summer with my dear friends Sara and Gerald Murphy, an American couple who live there, in their sun-filled, seaside house."

He looked at Alice.

"When I was a young man, American parents of great fortune sometimes took their children on trips to learn about art and places and people all around the world," he told her. "It was called a grand tour. While we are not people of great fortune, I can proudly send you on this different sort of grand tour, at Mr. and Mrs. Murphy's home. Theirs is a magnificent, wondrous world. They knew your mother well, and loved her. And what's more, they have three smart, delightful children around your age."

Old Miss Pennyweather went pale. Her panic was now reaching a fever pitch.

"With due respect, sir, do you think this is the right cure for Miss Alice?" she asked. "After all, France is so very, *very* far away, and what if she should fall ill on the journey across the ocean, or worse, fall *into* the ocean, and—"

Mr. Atherton cleared his throat and looked sternly at the governess over the top of his glasses.

"Yes, Miss Pennyweather, I'm quite certain," he

said. "Sara and Gerald are the kindest and most nurturing people I know. Alice, your mother adored them, and they adored her."

Mr. Atherton took Alice's hands in his.

"You do need to know," he told her, "that Mr. and Mrs. Murphy are not like anyone you've ever met before, and their friends are all very . . . well, *unusual.* Once again, I'm asking you: Do you feel brave enough for this adventure?"

But his eyes looked mischievous instead of solemn, and so Alice felt deep down inside herself that she *was* indeed brave enough—just as her mother would have been brave enough—and she told him so.

"That's settled, then," he said, and sat back and put his pipe into his mouth. Old Miss Pennyweather looked as though she'd just swallowed a putrid-tasting bug.

Three weeks later, Alice and the governess and their travel trunks found themselves churning east across the Atlantic Ocean on a massive transatlantic liner named, aptly enough, the HMS *Sojourn.*

As Mr. Atherton watched the ship pull out of the harbor, he felt a pang about sending Alice so far away, and dreaded the loneliness of their house back on Gramercy Park. But as he had assured Old Miss

Pennyweather, he was indeed certain that the Murphys would be the right cure for Alice. To get over death, he believed, we need to be around life. After her mother's death, Alice herself would have to learn how to be truly alive and love life again. While Mr. Atherton was not certain about many things in life, he was certain about this: Sara and Gerald Murphy and their friends knew more about the art of living fully than just about anyone else.

Chapter Two

VILLA AMERICA

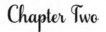

"OH DEAR," MOANED OLD MISS PENNYWEATHER AS
their train swayed from side to side. "I think I am going
to faint again. Alice, do ring for that beastly porter."

Alice pressed a buzzer to summon the porter. Ten
minutes later, the door to their car opened, and the
train's French porter stepped neatly inside. Alice liked
him. He had a funny little mustache that curlicued
away from his nose, and a skinny arrow of a beard
that pointed straight down toward his shoes. Already
he had been summoned four times to tend to Old Miss
Pennyweather's various ailments.

"Oui, madame?" he said wearily.

Old Miss Pennyweather, who had been lying back
on a couch with a handkerchief over her face, sat up
weakly.

"Just how much longer until we reach Antibes?" she asked the porter. "I feel as though we've been on this journey for *years*."

"We've only been on it for six hours," Alice pointed out, but her comment was not well received. Their train was chugging south from Paris, the capital of France, down to Antibes, the sleepy seaside town where Gerald and Sara Murphy and their three children lived.

"Madame will only need to endure the train for another two hours," the porter informed her.

"Two hours!" shrieked Old Miss Pennyweather. "I shall surely be dead by then."

"Should I bring more tea, Madame?" he asked her.

Old Miss Pennyweather nodded miserably. "It's the least you can do," she whimpered.

The porter turned to Alice. "And a chocolat chaud for Mademoiselle?" he whispered to her discreetly.

"Oui, please," Alice whispered back. Before leaving the car, the porter twitched his curly mustache in a funny way at Alice, who smiled a little.

Poor Old Miss Pennyweather lay back again and dropped her hankie back over her face. To be fair to the beaky governess, it had been a long journey from New York City. First, there had been the week on their ocean liner to England. The weather had been nasty, and huge waves had tossed the boat about like a toy in a tub. Within their first hour at sea, Old Miss Penny-weather's face had turned pea green, and she had taken to her bed for most of the rest of the trip.

Before they left New York, Alice had been certain that she would be scared on the journey. But so far, it had been exciting—even though Old Miss Penny-weather hadn't let her out of her sight for a second. On the ship to England, Alice had largely been confined to their cabin—except for her morning and afternoon "airings," in which Old Miss Pennyweather had bundled Alice up and marched her around the ship's decks. Alice swore that the governess slept with one eye open, to observe her charge at all times.

Terra firma proved to be no less traumatic for the governess. Old Miss Pennyweather and Alice stayed in London for a week to recover before moving on to France. London's fog had immediately inspired dark suspicions in Old Miss Pennyweather.

"It must be filled with all sorts of hideous things— not fit for breathing," she concluded. The hankie was once again fished out of her bag and affixed to her face.

Alice was not once allowed to leave their hotel. If she had been with her mother, and not the governess, they would have gone to Big Ben, Westminster Hall, the Tower of London, and Regent's Park—all in one morning. Her mother likely would even have figured out how to have tea with King George and Queen Mary, even if they'd had to scale the walls of Buckingham Palace to do so. As Alice languished under the beady eyes of Old Miss Pennyweather, she began to wonder if her father had made a mistake in sending her on this trip. So far, it seemed as though Old Miss Pennyweather had managed to bring the black clock shroud from Gramercy Park and cover everything with it.

To get to Paris, they had to take a train, another boat, and then another train. Old Miss Pennyweather quickly discovered that there was a great deal to dislike about Paris as well. The bathrooms appalled her. The unpasteurized milk was a death threat. People sat outside at cafés. ("Eating on the street!" Old Miss Pennyweather cried. "Why use plates at all? Just eat off the pavement, why don't you.") French dog owners did not clean up after their dogs. ("Re*volt*ing," she sniffed. "Paris is the most uncivilized place in the world.") Alice, on the other hand, found Paris to be perfectly delightful—especially once you learned to look where you stepped.

And now, on this final train to Antibes, Old Miss

Pennyweather kept the windows firmly shut and even closed all the curtains—to guard Alice, she said, from being "absolutely blinded by that dreadful Mediterranean sun."

At last Old Miss Pennyweather seemed to fall into a fitful sleep under her hankie, giving off choppy little snores. Alice sneaked a look through the curtains. When they left New York, a dark slush had still coated the city. But here in springtime France, the train wound through fields thick with French tulips. Alice would have given anything at that moment to be out in that warm sea of flowers, picking great bundles of them and feeling the sun on her face. Instead, she contented herself with watching the countryside speed by until Old Miss Pennyweather woke up with a snort. Smacking her lips, she sat up, stretched, and then fished from her satchel a newspaper clipping, given to her by Mr. Atherton before they left New York.

"Let's inspect these beastly eccentrics with whom we will be staying," she said.

Alice stood next to Old Miss Pennyweather and together they examined the clipping, which included a grainy photograph of Mr. and Mrs. Murphy.

"Why is Gerald wearing a sword?" Alice asked. "And why is Sara's pearl necklace so long?"

"*Just* a moment, young lady," snapped Old Miss Pennyweather. "You will refer to them as Mr. and Mrs. Murphy—not Gerald and Sara. And as to why he is wearing a sword: I simply cannot answer that question. And who *knows* what their children are like. Probably just as odd, I'm sure of it."

She shook her head.

"Oh dear, just *look* at them," she said, patting her damp cheeks with the hankie. "Read what it says here in the article: 'Mr. Gerald and Sara Murphy are friends with some of the most innovative artists and musicians in Paris.' I certainly know what that means, and I heartily disapprove."

"What does it mean?" asked Alice.

"It means," thundered Old Miss Pennyweather, "that your father is sending us to live for the next few months among hooligans, communists, and anarchists."

Alice looked at the clipping again.

"I don't see anything about hooligans or anarchists," she said. "Just artists and musicians."

This reassurance only made Old Miss Pennyweather whimper.

"What are hooligans and anarchists, anyway?" pressed Alice.

"Oh, *do* be quiet," said Old Miss Pennyweather, rubbing her eyes. After a minute, she rose again and, with great, heroic effect, pulled some books out of her bag.

"We'll simply have to do the best we can, Alice," she said. "I shall do my utmost to shield you from the onslaught of peculiarity and indignity that we are certain to endure. We will share a home with these Murphys for the duration of this so-called grand tour, as your father instructed. But I will make sure that we live apart from them as much as possible, and we shall continue with our routines. I will give you your regular lessons daily—beginning now."

Old Miss Pennyweather seemed fortified after delivering this rousing speech, and sitting up very straight now, she began to read from a grammar book.

"Lesson nine," she said, pointing straight into the air. "Prepositions and prepositional phrases."

Alice picked up the newspaper clipping again. As usual, she heard Old Miss Pennyweather's voice but didn't listen to the words. She looked at the photo of Mr. and Mrs. Murphy. Something about them warmed the winter cold that still seemed to be lingering inside Alice.

"A prepositional phrase is a modifying phrase

consisting of a preposition and its object," Old Miss Pennyweather read.

Alice lay back on the cushions on the couch, still holding the clipping. A light breeze came in from behind the drawn curtains, and the clipping fluttered in her fingers as though it were dancing. The sight pleased Alice. The train rocked from side to side, and soon she fell asleep.

⟡

AN HOUR LATER, there was a knock at the compartment door. The porter peeked in.

"Madame, we are arriving in Antibes," he said.

"Oh, thank merciful God!" cried Old Miss Pennyweather. "Alice, wake up this instant."

Porters heaved the passengers' trunks and satchels out of their compartments onto the platform outside. Old Miss Pennyweather straightened her hat and began raking a comb through Alice's hair.

"Remember to stand up straight," she instructed. "When you greet Mr. and Mrs. Murphy, please say, 'How do you do,' and then stand back! Leave the rest to me. Oh dear, oh dear—I wonder if you're meant to curtsy to them. They're only Americans, but this *is*

Europe. You had better curtsy, just to be safe." She looked Alice over, from head to toe. "Oh, Alice, please take off that brooch. You might lose it."

"No," said Alice, covering it up with her hand.

"Hand it over, young lady," said Old Miss Pennyweather.

"I won't," said Alice, who was usually a very obedient child.

"Last call for Antibes," called the porter from the platform outside.

"Oh, hurry," cried Old Miss Pennyweather, forgetting the battle of the brooch. They hurried off the train onto the platform.

Alice squinted in the bright sunlight and looked around for a man wearing a sword and a woman in a waist-long pearl necklace. Passengers drifted off the platform to waiting automobiles and horse-drawn carriages in front of the tiny station. Soon the platform was empty. The train pulled away from the station, bearing a now-very-happy French porter inside.

"Well, I never!" exclaimed Old Miss Pennyweather, coughing and waving her hankie about to clear the dust. "Where on earth *are* they? Surely they got my telegram with our arrival details."

A gnarled-looking man in overalls and a straw hat

trotted out onto the platform, and approached Old Miss Pennyweather and Alice.

"Madame Pen-ee-weather et Mademoiselle Aleece?" he said.

Old Miss Pennyweather glared at him suspiciously.

"Yes, I am Miss Prudence Pennyweather, and this is my charge, Miss Alice Atherton of the New York Athertons," she said wrathfully. "Who are you?"

"Gaston," he said, pointing to himself. "Jardinier pour Monsieur et Madame Murphy. You come now."

Old Miss Pennyweather whipped out her phrase book and looked up the word *jardinier.*

"A gardener!" she cried. "The Murphys sent their *gardener* to retrieve us, instead of coming to get us themselves? I've never heard of such terrible manners."

Gaston dragged their travel trunks to a wagon nearby and hauled them up into the back. He gestured toward a plank seat in the back of the wagon with the world's flattest pillow across it. Two hefty donkeys were harnessed to the front of the wagon.

"Sit, please," Gaston told Old Miss Pennyweather and Alice.

Old Miss Pennyweather, ornery and dazed but without options, lumbered up into the wagon. Alice

climbed in after her. It was nothing like her city carriage back home, but she immediately liked being in
the wagon. For once, there were no windows for Old
Miss Pennyweather to close or curtains for her to draw.
The sun felt warm on Alice's face.

Gaston climbed into the driver's seat up front. He
flicked the donkeys with a strap, and the wagon shot
forward. Old Miss Pennyweather let out a squawk,
grabbed Alice, and smothered the girl's face into her
bosom. Alice tried to wiggle free, but Old Miss Pennyweather held tight.

The road curved left and then right, and soon it followed along a cliff above the deep blue Mediterranean
Sea. The wagon *bump-bump-bump*ed upward as the
cliff road went higher and higher. Old Miss Pennyweather released Alice and concerned herself with
rapping Gaston with her parasol instead.

"Slow down—you'll kill us all!" she shrieked, but
Gaston just hunched over and weathered the parasol
*whack*s. He flicked the straps again, and the donkeys
cantered even faster.

Suddenly, as the wagon went around a corner, Alice
gasped.

"Look, Miss Pennyweather!" she cried, pointing.

There, at the top of the cliff, stood a big, beautiful

house, gleaming in the sunshine. White fringed awnings hung above all of the windows, reminding Alice of heavy eyelids shading sleepy eyes. An orchard of fruit trees surrounded the house, their flowers so fragrant that Alice could practically taste the bright oranges and lemons dangling from the branches. Gaston withstood one more *whack!* of the Pennyweather parasol before turning to face the ladies.

"Villa America," he told them, pointing at the house. "The Murphy house."

The donkeys lurched forward and barreled up a steep, winding driveway toward the villa. Olive trees and fruit trees canopied the way, some of the branches so heavy with fruit that a fat, low-hanging lemon *wump*ed Old Miss Pennyweather right between the eyes.

When they reached the top of the hill, Gaston steered around to the back of the house and stopped the donkeys. The wagon now stood alongside a vast, sunny terrace made from white and gray marble tiles, which looked to Alice like a chessboard. Bumblebees buzzed in the flowers of the fruit trees around the house.

Old Miss Pennyweather stood up unsteadily.

"Where on *earth* are the Murphys?" she cried.

Gaston pointed toward the end of the terrace. There, fast asleep on a wicker settee, lay a man in a striped shirt and white shorts, his face hidden under a bright white hat with a wide brim.

"Monsieur Murphy," reported the gardener.

"Asleep in the middle of the day!" gasped Old Miss Pennyweather. "And outside in all of this heat, probably full of wine. Dressed like a sailor, no less. Alice, you stay right here while I investigate the matter."

She pointed her parasol at Gaston.

"You," she added. "Please stay right where you are. You'll likely be taking us straight back to the train station in a moment."

Alice watched as Old Miss Pennyweather approached the sleeping man.

"Ahem," said the governess crossly.

The man did not stir.

"A-HEM," said Old Miss Pennyweather, quite noisily this time.

Still no response.

Old Miss Pennyweather gave the man a little nudge on the shoulder with her parasol. Suddenly he sat straight up, his hat falling from his face onto the ground.

"Good God, woman—can't you see that I'm trying

to sleep?" he exclaimed. "You're ruining the best nap-ping hour of the day."

"Well!" huffed Old Miss Pennyweather. "Are you or are you not Mr. Gerald Murphy?"

"I am indeed Mr. Gerald Murphy," he said, glaring at her. "And who the devil are you?"

Then he saw Alice standing there.

"Oh!" he cried. "Oh! Is it really—? It's not Friday already, is it? The days *do* blend together so. You must be Alice."

He stood up and marched over to her, then threw his arms around her in a great, crushing hug. Old Miss Pennyweather gasped, but Alice didn't mind the embrace. Mr. Murphy smelled of sandalwood, and it had been weeks since anyone had hugged her.

"You're wearing the sword!" she cried happily when he finally released her. "We saw a photograph of it in a newspaper."

"I always wear my sword," he told her. "You never know when pirates might arrive," he added, pointing in the direction of the sea. "One must be ready to fend them off."

Alice was incredulous.

"Pirates are only in fairy tales," she said. And then, more uncertainly: "Aren't they?"

Mr. Murphy looked at her solemnly.

"Well, Alice, I'll let you in on an important secret," he said. "Our cook makes the best gooseberry jam ever created, and it has magical properties. It is made from gooseberries grown in a hidden part of our very own garden, right here at Villa America. Anyone who eats a spoonful of this magical jam stays young forever. Or forever-ish, anyway."

"What hogwash," cried Old Miss Pennyweather. "We've only been here for a minute, and you are already filling this child's head with nonsense. I knew that Mr. Atherton was mad to send us here."

Mr. Murphy cheerfully ignored her.

"This jam has become very famous all over the world," he continued. "And naturally, *everyone* wants a jar, but we simply won't part with it. So evil kings and wicked Hollywood movie stars and vain society ladies send pirate ships from all around the globe to try to steal the gooseberry jam from us. And *that,* Alice Atherton, is why I need this sword."

"Gerald," called a voice from inside the house. "Have our guests arrived?"

The door opened and a woman emerged. Wearing a flowing white dress, she was so serene that she almost appeared to be floating. A long strand of pearls dangled from her neck, shimmering in the sun as she walked.

"Oh, you *are* here," the woman said, and like Mr. Murphy, she came over to Alice and gave her a warm hug. She looked into Alice's eyes. "I am Sara Murphy. Welcome to Villa America, darling girl. We are so pleased that you chose to spend the summer with us. My goodness, you look so much like your mother. I knew her from when we were young girls—did your father tell you that? She was always climbing trees and getting into scrapes and trouble. I just *adored* her. You have her eyes."

She straightened up.

"Children," she called. "Alice is here. Come quickly, please!"

Alice heard a chorus of great shrieks and whoops. The house door swung open, and out tumbled two young boys and one young girl in bathing costumes.

"Wait—we forgot Mistigris!" yelled the smaller boy, and he ran back inside. The other two children ran over to Alice.

"I'm Baoth," said one of them, a boy who looked a few years younger than Alice.

"I'm Honoria," said the girl, who was around Alice's age. "Oh, it's so hot outside. Why don't you take off your travel clothes and come swimming with us? We're going down to the sea."

The other little boy burst back out onto the terrace, carrying a small monkey.

"I'm Patrick," he said. "And this is Mistigris! Say hello, Mistigris!"

He tried to hand the monkey to Alice.

"Ahhh!" screamed Old Miss Pennyweather. "Oh, feral beast—a single bite!—the end of us—" she sputtered, and then she fainted right onto the terrace.

"Oh dear," exclaimed Mrs. Murphy. "What a terrible first impression we have made. The poor thing must be absolutely exhausted from that long journey. Gerald, can you and Gaston carry her up to her room? Alice, why don't you go along with them? You can wash up and change. We'll send up some lunch shortly."

Mr. Murphy and Gaston lugged Old Miss Pennyweather into the house. The governess's hankie had fallen onto the terrace when she fainted, and the monkey was now playing with it. Alice smiled at the sight, and followed the men into the house.

"Bye, Alice!" shouted Patrick. "See you at dinner. Listen for the gong! That's how you know dinner's ready."

The monkey let out a gleeful shriek. As Alice went

inside, she glanced shyly back at the family standing there on the terrace in the sunshine. Patrick waved encouragingly at her. She felt so strange inside. It wasn't until she got upstairs that she identified the feeling as a faint combination of happiness and hope. It had been so long since she'd felt either that she hadn't recognized them when they returned.

❧

MR. MURPHY AND GASTON placed Old Miss Pennyweather on a bed in an upstairs bedroom, and left to give her some privacy. Alice sat on a chair in the corner and waited for her governess to wake up.

A knock came on the door.

"Come in," called Alice.

A young woman in a crisp linen maid's uniform bustled into the room, carrying a tray covered with plates of fruit, bread, and butter, and a jug of water.

"Allo, Mademoiselle. I am Isabelle," she said as she set down the tray on a desk and began opening the window shutters. "She is having quite a sleep, no?" she added, glancing down at Old Miss Pennyweather. Alice giggled.

Outside the windows glimmered the vast sea. A breeze rushed into the room and fluttered the edges of

Old Miss Pennyweather's pillow. Suddenly the governess gave a terrific snort and sat straight up. She looked at Isabelle, who had begun unpacking Old Miss Pennyweather's trunk and hanging up her dresses.

"Stop right there," she thundered. "Do not unpack another item. We are leaving this instant."

Alice was about to eat a fresh fig from the tray when Old Miss Pennyweather cried: "Put that down at once! We have no idea where it came from. Has it even been *washed*?"

"Why, Madame, most of it came from Villa America's own orchards," said Isabelle, surprised.

Old Miss Pennyweather rose out of the bed and straightened her clothes.

"Please tell Mr. and Mrs. Murphy that I wish to have a word with them, privately and immediately," she told Isabelle, who nodded and quietly left. "Alice, we will be leaving shortly, as soon as I finish my conversation with these depraved hedonists."

She swept out of the room.

"Psssst," Alice heard from the hallway, and one of the Murphy boys peeked through the doorway. "It's me, Patrick," he said, coming into the room. He had been hastily reclad in a crisp sailor shirt and shorts. "I'm six."

The other boy, Baoth, followed him. He too had been stuffed into more formal clothing, and looked none too happy about it.

"I'm eight and ten months," he informed Alice. "That's also eight and five-sixths."

"And I'm ten," said their sister, Honoria, who followed them in. Her white dress fluttered prettily. She was exactly as tall as Alice. "How old are you?"

"I'm ten too," said Alice.

"It's good that you're here," Honoria told her. "I've been outnumbered for years. Now it's two girls against two boys."

"Do you have any brothers or sisters?" Patrick asked, helping himself to the bread and butter.

"None," replied Alice.

"Our mother said your mother died, and that's why you came here," said Patrick.

Suddenly Alice felt the icy New York City winter come back inside her. She had thought that the French sunshine and breeze had started to thaw it out of her, but she could see that she had been fooling herself. The winter feeling had just been hiding. Maybe it would always be there, like a snake with its cold blood, waiting for an opportunity to wrap itself around her.

"I only wanted to say," said Patrick obliviously, his

mouth full, "that we can share our mother with you, if you want. She's awfully nice."

Baoth went to the door and listened for a moment.

"Your horrid governess is talking to our parents downstairs," he whispered, waving at Alice. "Come here."

The four children tiptoed out of the room and sat down at the top of the stairs quietly, eavesdropping on the conversation below.

"Oh, Miss Pennyweather," said Mrs. Murphy. "I'm so relieved to see you up and about. It must have been such an exhausting journey."

"Would you like a sherry?" asked Mr. Murphy. "Or something stronger, perhaps."

"No, thank you," snapped Old Miss Pennyweather, and Alice could imagine her face at that moment. The governess was probably wearing what Alice privately called her hawk look, in which Old Miss Pennyweather stared down her beaky nose like a hawk sizing up its prey. "I would simply like to inform you that we plan on leaving again immediately."

"Oh," said Mrs. Murphy after a moment. "We're so sorry to hear that."

"Yes, *dreadfully* sorry," added Mr. Murphy. "May I ask why you are planning to depart so swiftly?"

"This household is no place for an impressionable young girl," sniffed Old Miss Pennyweather. "In the brief time since we arrived, Alice has already been subjected to alarming fibs, a herd of near-naked children, a rabid animal, and a most unhygienic offering of food."

At this, the Murphy children giggled and poked each other.

"You're the rabid animal," whispered Baoth to Patrick.

"What? *You* are. The stinkiest rabid animal ever."

"No—I'm the alarming fib."

"Be *quiet,*" hissed Honoria. "We're missing the good part."

"I'm certain that Mr. Atherton had no accurate idea what sort of a family this is," continued Old Miss Pennyweather. "A summer here would give that child a most unholy education."

Mr. Murphy laughed out loud. It was a sharp burst of laughter that reminded Alice of a dog's bark.

"Please book us on the first available train back to Paris," instructed Old Miss Pennyweather.

"Well," said Mr. Murphy, still chuckling. "I'm afraid that there isn't a train for two more days. This is just a tiny town in the middle of nowhere, during the off-season. It's one of the reasons we live here, after all: to get away from people. So I'm afraid that you're stuck here for now."

"Horrors!" wailed Old Miss Pennyweather. "Well, in that case, we shall confine ourselves to our rooms until we can leave."

And with that, she paraded out of the living room, her nose in the air.

The children shot up from the top stair. In the hurry, Patrick tripped on his own feet, fell down right on his face, and bloodied his nose. As the governess stomped up the stairs, the Murphy children ran down the hallway.

Old Miss Pennyweather blanched when she saw the drops of Patrick's blood on the floor. And true to her word, for the next two days, she kept Alice upstairs in their big room, shutters closed. They continued their lessons, as usual. Isabelle brought them meals on trays. Alice could often hear the Murphy children playing in the gardens or on the terrace outside, and she longed to join them. She had only just arrived, but already sensed that perhaps her father had been right after all: there *did* seem to be something magical about this family and this place and maybe even the monkey. And now the governess was about to take it all away. If only she could send a letter to her father and ask him to intervene, but there wasn't enough time.

Two days later, Old Miss Pennyweather had their trunks packed and ready to go. She marched Alice downstairs triumphantly.

Mr. and Mrs. Murphy were waiting for them in the living room. The walls, ceiling, and floors were bright white, and all the furniture had been upholstered with black satin. Alice had never seen another room like it.

"We are ready to be taken to the station," declared Old Miss Pennyweather. "Might we trouble Gaston to pack up the wagon?"

"Just a moment, please," said Mr. Murphy, holding up his hand. "We have some news."

He unfolded a telegram.

"*You,* dear Miss Pennyweather, will be leaving today," he said. "But Miss Alice will be staying with us. That is, if she chooses to." Alice's heart leaped.

"What on earth are you talking about?" said Old Miss Pennyweather.

"These are instructions from the child's father himself," said Mr. Murphy. "Right after you arrived, I sent Mr. Atherton a telegram, explaining the situation and that you intended to return to New York immediately with Alice. I received a telegram back from him just now, and here it is."

He handed it to Old Miss Pennyweather. It read:

MURPHY STOP OH DEAR STOP
SEND PENNYWEATHER HOME
RIGHT AWAY STOP ALICE TO
REMAIN WITH YOU AND FAMILY
STOP I TRUST YOU AND SARA
ENTIRELY STOP ARCHIBALD

Old Miss Pennyweather stood there, speechless and white as milk. Alice was filled with love for her father: she hadn't even had to send him a letter. He just *knew*.

Mrs. Murphy kneeled beside Alice.

"Alice, your father wants you to stay with us this summer after all," she said. "But it's your choice, of course. I know that we feel like strangers to you now, but our families have known each other for a very long time. We will do our best to be a wonderful family to you during these summer months."

Alice looked at Old Miss Pennyweather and then she looked at the Murphys. The three children were now standing in the doorway, watching with great anticipation to see what would happen next.

"I want to stay," Alice said quietly.

And *this* is what happened next: Old Miss Penny-weather burst into tears and created quite a spectacle. Then she was carted away to the train station by poor Gaston. Mrs. Murphy, who actually felt sorry for the joyless governess, had kindly packed a picnic basket for Old Miss Pennyweather's train ride back to Paris, full of beautiful fruit from the Villa America orchards.

As the wagon disappeared around the bend, Patrick took Alice's hand.

"Now you can come out of your room at last," he told her.

A loud *bonnnnnggggg* sounded from the garden.

"Dinner!" shouted all three of the Murphy children. Patrick pulled Alice across the terrace, where a long table had been set up under the boughs of a swaying, flower-covered silver linden tree. Isabelle and Mrs. Murphy carried bowls filled with potatoes gleaming with melted butter, and bright ruby-red tomatoes; after that came a tray bearing a great, silvery fish, covered in lemons and salt.

The children scampered onto wood benches lining either side of the table, and Mr. and Mrs. Murphy sat down in chairs at the far ends. Alice hesitated.

"Is everything all right, Alice?" asked Mrs. Murphy. "Please join us."

"Am I allowed?" Alice asked. After all, she was

rarely permitted to sit at a dining table with grown-ups at home. Rather, she had eaten most of her meals in her room or the kitchen with Old Miss Pennyweather.

"Why, of course you are!" exclaimed Mrs. Murphy. "Please come sit right here, next to me."

Alice sat down. She felt strangely light, like a kite that had been released into the sky. It was a strange, entirely new feeling.

Mr. Murphy poured a glass of wine for himself and stood up.

"I'd like to propose a toast to our guest—no, to the newest member of our family—Miss Alice Atherton. Here's to you, Alice. And to unholy educations, as dear Miss Pennyweather put it."

"Oh, sit down, Gerald," said Mrs. Murphy.

"I have to say, Sara," said Mr. Murphy to his wife, "that Miss Pennyweather inadvertently gave me a rather brilliant idea. I have just realized that, during these coming weeks and months, we have the opportunity to give the children an education unlike any other. To that end, I have some highly unusual lessons and teachers in mind."

"What?" shrieked Patrick. "Who wants school in the middle of summer? I won't do it."

"Oh, hush," Mr. Murphy said. "I certainly don't

mean multiplication tables or grammar lessons. I have
something else in mind—something exciting and orig-
inal. Tomorrow, I'll begin making arrangements."

He sat back down and smiled happily.

"Children," he told them, "this is going to be a
summer to remember."

Chapter Three

THE WELCOME WISH

ALICE STARTLED WHEN SHE WOKE UP THE NEXT morning. She heard the unfamiliar sound of the sea outside her window, and then the sounds of the children already whooping and playing in the garden.

She lay in bed and wondered what she was supposed to do. Back in New York, Old Miss Pennyweather had come into her room every morning to wake her up and help her get dressed. Here at Villa America, was Alice supposed to get up and go downstairs, or would the Murphys think it rude and demanding if she just materialized in the kitchen, waiting to be fed? Best to wait for them to come and get her, she decided.

Half an hour later, Alice had grown hungry. Her stomach rumbled but she didn't leave her room, still unsure of what was expected of her.

Her bedroom door banged opened, and the three Murphy children burst in.

"Why on earth are you still in bed?" cried Patrick. "We've been waiting forever for you to get up. The donkeys are waiting. Come on!"

Alice got out of bed and stood there in her nightgown.

"Donkeys?" she said.

"We ride them to the beach," said Honoria. "Hurry up and put on a play dress."

"What's a play dress?" Alice asked.

"You *must* have one," said Honoria, and together the girls looked through Alice's dresses, now hanging neatly in a wardrobe. All of them were fancy and stiff and better suited to a parlor than a beach.

"Oh, you can't play in *those,*" scoffed Honoria. "You can just borrow one of mine." She ran to her room and came back with a simple white linen dress. "Put this on, and meet us downstairs on the terrace."

"But who is going to help dress me?" asked Alice, holding the dress uncertainly.

Honoria looked at her, confused.

"Dress you?" she said. "You just pull it down over your head."

"Oh, I see," said Alice, and her face pinkened with

mild embarrassment. Her stomach growled again. "Um—is there anything to eat?"

"We eat breakfast at the beach," Patrick told her as Honoria herded him and Baoth toward the door. "And on the way, too. You'll see—" he called back as the door closed.

Alice took off her nightgown and pulled on Honoria's dress. She stood in front of the mirror. The dress was airy and light, and she felt airy and light in it. Then she pinned her mother's lilies-of-the-valley brooch onto the dress, laced up her boots, and ran downstairs.

Out on the terrace, Mrs. Murphy was helping the children climb up onto the backs of two gray donkeys, who stood patiently as they were loaded up. Baoth and Patrick perched on top of one donkey, Honoria on the other.

"Why are you wearing those boots, silly?" called Baoth. Alice saw then that all three Murphy children had bare feet, and so she sheepishly took off her boots. She had never been outside without shoes on. The marble-tiled terrace felt smooth and sun-warmed under her feet.

"And why are you wearing that fancy pin?" asked Patrick.

"I almost always wear it," said Alice evasively.

"Why?" Patrick pressed.

Mrs. Murphy bustled over to Alice.

"It's a beautiful brooch, and I remember your mother wearing it," she said. "Just take care that you don't lose it on the beach. Baoth, don't let Patrick slip off. Let me help you now, Alice: you can share Honoria's donkey."

She guided Alice up onto the donkey's bare back.

"Put your arms around my waist," Honoria told her. "You won't fall."

The donkeys moved forward. Alice couldn't help letting out a shriek, a mix of joy and fear. As the little caravan passed under the fruit trees on the winding road down to the sea, the children reached up and pulled fruit off the branches.

"For breakfast," called Baoth. "Grab one!"

Keeping one arm around Honoria, Alice grabbed a fat, juicy apricot. She bit into it.

"Oh no," she cried. "I got juice on your dress, Honoria."

"That doesn't matter—look at mine," said Honoria, twisting around to show Alice the front of her dress, also covered with apricot juice. The girls pulled down more fruit from trees as they passed under them— oranges and figs—and bunched it up in their dresses.

Soon they arrived at a small, crescent-shaped beach, mostly covered in heaps of dark green seaweed. Alice had only been to a wide, flat beach before, with the fierce, cold blue waves of the Atlantic Ocean thundering on the sand. This beach—with its gently lapping, warm emerald-green waves—felt intimate and kind, somehow.

Mr. Murphy was already down on the beach, clearing some of the seaweed away. His belted sword glinted in the morning sun.

"Dow-Dow!" the children shrieked. This was their nickname for their father.

"Hurry up," he called to them. "The seaweed monster is devouring the entire beach. I need your help—quickly."

The children slid off the donkeys and tethered them in the shade of a grove of trees.

"What seaweed monster?" asked Alice.

"Why, this one," said Gerald, pointing to an especially large heap of seaweed on the sand.

"But," said Alice, "that's just seaweed that washed up there."

"No, it's a monster," said Patrick. "Can't you *see*?" He ran over to Alice and whispered in her ear. "Dow-Dow thinks it's a real monster, Alice. Don't tell him the truth. He would be terribly disappointed."

"Oh," said Alice, relieved. "It's a game."

"Yes," Patrick told her. "We have to clear all the seaweed away, and once we banish the monster, we eat breakfast."

The children scattered across the beach and dragged the seaweed across the sand, dumping it into a big pile. It was cold and slimy, but the children shouted with glee while they worked. Soon they were covered in sand. Patrick and Baoth and Honoria ran straight into the sea, still in their play clothes.

"Come in, Alice," yelled Patrick.

Alice grew embarrassed. She stood politely at the water's edge and washed off her hands and face.

"Maybe after breakfast," she told him.

Mr. Murphy spread out a picnic blanket, and the children joined him there for a morning feast. In addition to the fruit that the children had gathered, Mr. Murphy had brought a picnic basket filled with bread, butter, and cheese.

"Dow-Dow," said Patrick, "I think I just saw the seaweed monster move. It's going to eat our breakfast!"

"You know," said Mr. Murphy, standing up, "seaweed monsters *love* cheese. We'd better act fast."

And with that, he stalked over to the seaweed pile and plunged his sword right into the middle of it. Alice screamed before she remembered that it wasn't a real seaweed monster, and the other children laughed.

"Olé!" cried Mr. Murphy, coming back to the picnic blanket. "This reminds me, children," he said, picking up an orange, "that our first teacher of summer arrives tomorrow morning. Today is your last day at liberty, so make the most of it, my darlings."

"Can we take Alice into town to see a moving picture?" asked Honoria.

"Yes, you may," said Mr. Murphy. "I'm sure that Gaston would welcome the chance to visit his favorite tobacco shop anyway."

Late that morning, Gaston took them into the town center. It reminded Alice of an old fort, filled with its pretty stone buildings and the craggy stone wall encircling the town center. Gaston steered the wagon into the main square. The children leaped off the back.

"I will come back for you at four o'clock," Gaston told them, and he drove back down the street.

A church tower's bell chimed twelve times.

"Hurry!" cried Baoth. "The moving picture is starting!"

The children ran up to a rather decrepit-looking stone building and bought four tickets from an old man sitting drowsily on a wooden chair by the front doorway. Inside, in a large, hot room, were rows of wooden chairs. An oversized white sheet had been stretched across the front wall. Dozens of people sat, cooling themselves with fan-palm leaves and eating peanuts, throwing the shells onto the ground. Only three chairs remained empty, way in the back of the room. Patrick had to sit on Honoria's lap.

"It smells like feet in here," complained Baoth.

"It always smells like feet," said Patrick cheerfully. "I kind of like it."

Alice leaned toward Honoria. "What happens next?"

"Well, the show begins," she said.

"But there's no stage," said Alice.

All three Murphy children stared at her.

"You've never been to the moving pictures before?" exclaimed Baoth. "The show happens there, on the sheet!"

Just then, the ceiling light—a single bulb hanging from a wire—went out, and the old ticket seller shambled down to the front of the room. He sat at a ramshackle piano, and as he began to play a funny little tune, suddenly the wall sheet lit up and a moving drawing appeared on it. Alice was stunned.

"What *is* that?" she asked.

"It's Felix the Cat," Patrick told her. "A cartoon."

"But the drawing is *moving,*" cried Alice, pointing.

"That's why it's called a moving picture, silly," Baoth said. "They probably have them in New York too, you know."

Alice stared up at the movie with pure glee. Felix the Cat was busy pretending to be a suitcase so his owner would take him on a trip. Everyone in the theater laughed. A boy selling bags of peanuts approached the children.

"We only had enough money for the show," Honoria told him. "But we'll trade you some fruit from our garden." The boy took three figs and an orange in exchange for one bag of peanuts. After the cartoon ended, a new movie came on—this time with real people in it, like a photograph wondrously coming to life, Alice thought. The movie was about a young Indian prince who was secretly sent to live in America because a wicked man wanted to prevent him from becoming king of his country one day.

When the pianist thundered out an especially dramatic tune for a chase scene, he got so excited that he fell right off his chair. Everyone in the theater laughed. The embarrassed old man stood up grumpily and lumbered back toward the door. Everyone threw peanut shells at him for being a poor sport, but just as he was about to leave, Patrick ran up to him and grabbed his hand.

"Oh, please stay and keep playing," he said. "It's no good without you. And I'll help with the high notes, if you like."

The man smiled then, and squeezed Patrick's cheeks. Patrick led him back to the piano and everyone cheered and threw peanut shells again, this time to celebrate. It looked like the air was filled with confetti. Patrick stood next to the old man at the piano and plunked on the high notes when things got exciting again in the movie.

When it was all over, everyone filed out into the town square. It had been stiflingly hot in the movie theater, and some of the moviegoers splashed water from the town square's fountain onto their faces and necks. While they waited for Gaston, Alice and the Murphy children milled around the square. They looked longingly into the window of a pâtisserie. A woman wearing a white apron came out of the shop, holding a big pan of small, fresh butter cakes.

"Allo, Murphy children," she said, smiling. "How are you today?"

"Good afternoon, Madame Claudette," they said to her.

"And who is this?" she asked, nodding toward Alice.

"She's our long-lost sister," Baoth told her. "She was in a shipwreck out at sea and only just managed to swim back. We found her on the beach this morning."

"He's fibbing, as usual," said Honoria. "This is Alice Atherton from New York. She's staying with us for the whole summer."

"And getting an unholy education with us," Patrick chimed in. "That's what our papa said, anyway."

"Is that so?" said Madame Claudette, looking quizzically at Patrick. "Bienvenue, Mademoiselle Alice. Would you all like some butter cakes?"

"Yes, please," the children said, practically in unison, and crowded around her. Madame Claudette gave a cake to Alice, Honoria, and Patrick, but held the last one high up above Baoth's head.

"Monsieur Baoth, you will have to earn your gâteau after telling me that fib," she said, still smiling. "You can earn it with a dance."

Baoth looked pleased. He stepped into the square and took a bow. Honoria and Patrick clapped. Honoria leaned over to Alice.

"Watch this," she said. "Baoth loves singing and dancing more than anything in the world. He's pretty good, too."

Baoth began to sing.

It was an old fashioned garden
Just an old fashioned garden
But it carried me back
To that dear little shack
In the land of long ago . . .

He danced as he sang, and his feet made a pitter-patter drumbeat as he moved. Several people gathered around him in a circle as he performed. When he finished, they clapped, and he gave another bow. Smiling, Madame Claudette handed him a butter cake. A fancy lady wearing a big hat with feathers wobbled forward, leaning on a cane, and gave Baoth a coin.

"Use it to make a wish," Patrick said excitedly.

The children walked with Baoth over to the fountain. Just as he was about to throw the coin into the water, he stopped and held the coin out to Alice instead.

"You take it," he told her. "As a welcoming present."

Alice took the coin shyly. She held it for a moment, closed her eyes, and then threw it into the fountain.

"What did you wish for?" asked Patrick.

"No, don't tell us," Honoria said. "You're *never* supposed to say your wishes out loud. If you do, they don't come true. Everyone knows that."

Alice smiled and nibbled on her butter cake. She

had only been with the Murphy children in Antibes for a few days, but she already knew that she loved it there, and she suspected that she might already love them a little bit too. What she *did* know for certain: Alice already didn't want to leave Antibes and the Murphys and Villa America and go back to New York and Old Miss Pennyweather and the black-shrouded, ticking grandfather clock at her house.

And so with that coin, her welcome wish had been to somehow make this summer turn into forever.

Chapter Four

ART IS EVERYWHERE

WHEN SHE WOKE UP THE NEXT MORNING, ALICE
still felt happy—until she remembered that Mr. Murphy had said that lessons would begin today. She had never had lessons except those taught by Old Miss Pennyweather, and thinking about the governess and those dreary lessons made Alice feel cold inside again. That New York cold almost froze out the warmth of the delightful foot-smelling movie theater and the butter cakes and Baoth's dance in the square.

Someone pounded on her door, and then Patrick burst in.

"Get up, Alice," he told her. "Come downstairs. It's an emergency. But a good emergency."

Alice threw off her covers, put on her borrowed

play dress, and ran down the stairs after him out onto the terrace. There—on the middle of the table, surrounded by platters of fruit and bread and little boiled eggs—sat a strange, small man, cross-legged and wearing a striped shirt. On his head teetered a ragged top hat. Mistigris the monkey perched on his shoulder.

Honoria and Baoth ran out onto the terrace too.

"Pablo!" Honoria shouted.

"You are late to breakfast," he informed the children. "And so I am going to eat all of it." He grabbed fistfuls of grapes and began gobbling them.

"Save some for us," cried Patrick.

"You'd better hurry up here and get yours, then," he said. "I am very hungry this morning." And the man reached out, snatched up Patrick, and pretended to eat him up too. Patrick gave a scream of delight. Alice, not wishing to be devoured as well, sat warily on a chair at the far end of the table.

Mr. Murphy came out of the villa.

"Oh, how sad that Patrick is being eaten by a wild beast," he joked. "And just before his seventh birthday, too."

He stood next to Alice and put a hand on her shoulder.

"Alice, please meet our friend Señor Pablo Picasso

of Spain, by way of Paris," he said to her. "I'm afraid that even our monkey has better table manners than he does. But Señor Picasso's redeeming quality is that he makes art like no one else. And lucky you," Mr. Murphy told the children. "Señor Picasso is going to be your first teacher of the summer."

Señor Picasso pretended to spit out Patrick's foot.

"That is some very tough meat," he said. "And it needs salt and pepper."

The artist hopped off the table.

"It is time for this feast to end," he said, "and for another to begin. Except this time, it will be a feast for the eyes—and for the mind."

He took a deep bow, and the top hat plunked onto the terrace. Mistigris bowed as well. The children clapped.

"Now, sit in a row, little creatures," Señor Picasso instructed. "You too," he told Alice, who timidly took her place next to the Murphy children. She was still a bit scared of Señor Picasso, but she liked him also.

"I begin with a simple question," Señor Picasso said. "What is art?"

"A painting," suggested Honoria.

"A drawing," said Patrick, eating bread and butter, as usual.

"Something that hangs in a museum," Alice managed, thinking of the massive, echoing Metropolitan Museum back in New York City, which had room after room of gold-framed paintings of forests and mountains and saints rolling their eyes around.

"Hmmm, these are very revealing answers," said Señor Picasso. "Now, another question: What is art made out of?"

"Paint," answered Baoth. "On canvas."

"You can paint on paper, too," Honoria said. "And also draw, with pencils and charcoals."

Señor Picasso pointed his top hat at the children.

"While all of these answers are correct," he told them, "they have also made me sad. Very sad indeed."

"What?" asked Baoth. "Why would correct answers make you sad? Usually wrong answers are the ones that make teachers cross."

"Because those answers tell me a lot about the way that you look at the world," Señor Picasso replied. "Art is *everywhere,* not just hanging in a frame in some museum. It is all around us. Any object can be made into art, or used to make art. This branch," he said, seizing a low bough of the linden tree above him. "This napkin. That silly little monkey. *Anything.* Once you realize that, it will change the way you look at the world forever."

"I don't believe that," said Baoth. He picked up a spoon, a butter knife, and a fork. "How can you make art from these?"

"Watch," said Señor Picasso. He pulled a few strings from his shabby shirt, which was unraveling at the bottom. First, he tied the fork and spoon together, so that the spoon head was on top and the fork prongs looked like a short skirt at the bottom. Then he took two small fruit forks and tied them across the middle, their prongs facing in opposite directions.

"What does this look like?" he asked. The children were quiet for a moment.

"Well, to me," Alice ventured bravely, "it looks like a woman wearing a skirt. The spoon is her head, and the little forks are her arms and hands."

"Yes!" said Señor Picasso. "And you win the prize: a little metal dolly." He handed the tied-up utensils to her. "Now, stand back," he told the children. Señor Picasso then roughly pulled the white tablecloth out from under the food. Some fruit bounced down and across the terrace, and Mistigris chased it.

Señor Picasso spread the tablecloth across the terrace floor.

"Pass me that bowl of cherries," he told Honoria. He gave a cherry a nip with his teeth and, using it like a crayon, began to draw on the tablecloth. The children gathered around him, fascinated. Soon a drawing appeared.

"Look, it's us!" Patrick exclaimed.

"And Mistigris," said Baoth.

Alice stared at the tablecloth mural, and she too could see in those shapes four people and a mischievous monkey with a long tail.

"Now you try it," said Señor Picasso.

"Sara is not going to be very enthusiastic about this activity, Pablo," Mr. Murphy said from his bench under the silver linden tree, where he had been watching quietly. "She loves that tablecloth."

Alice kneeled over her part of the cloth with a cherry, feeling a little bit ridiculous. But then she found herself drawing with the fruit's juice, using the cherry as a pen of sorts.

"Time for the exhibit," called Señor Picasso a few minutes later. "Murphy, bring me a hammer and some nails."

When Mr. Murphy produced the tools, Señor Picasso messily ripped out each child's drawing, took each of the panels, and nailed the children's drawings to the fence surrounding the terrace. Honoria had drawn the sea. Baoth had drawn a boat. No one knew at first what Patrick had drawn, but he quickly clarified that the blotches of cherry juice on his panel were the seaweed monster from the beach. Alice had drawn a face.

"Who is that?" asked Honoria.

"Well," said Alice, embarrassed. "It's supposed to be me."

"You don't look at all well, Alice," said Patrick, and everyone laughed. Then Señor Picasso and Mr. Murphy paced in front of the cherry drawings and inspected them.

"I have to say," said Mr. Murphy, "that I think some important work has been done here."

"Yes, it's a start," announced Señor Picasso. "You are beginning to see that art can be made from any materials. Now we will expand on that lesson. Murphy, please call up your wagon. The children and I are going to their next classroom."

❧

AN HOUR LATER, Alice and the Murphy children found themselves back in Gaston's wagon with the donkeys hitched up. Señor Picasso sat up front with Gaston. Soon the wagon angled up a grassy hill and through a wall of pine trees, and then it stopped.

"We have arrived," said Señor Picasso grandly.

The children looked around in astonishment.

"But we're at the junkyard," exclaimed Honoria. "What does this have to do with art?"

"It has *everything* to do with art," said Señor Picasso, jumping off the wagon seat. "Come, follow me."

The children got off the wagon. In front of them stood vast piles of junk: broken bicycles, chipped porcelain sinks, brooms with frayed straw heads, cracked blue-and-white china dishes, three-legged chairs, and dressers with missing drawers. There were assorted old hats and shoes, some without laces, some without heels; stacks of long-forgotten books, magazines, and newspapers with torn pages; wild snarls of wires; glinting jumbles of scrap metal; and heaps of wood. An old automobile without wheels sullenly rusted away, pining for its days on the open road.

"Our job while we are here," Señor Picasso told the children, "is to collect objects with interesting shapes."

"But why?" asked Baoth, who was climbing into the driver's seat of the rusty car.

"Because we are going to bring them back to Villa America," said Señor Picasso, "and there, we are going to create sculptures from them."

"But you don't make sculptures from junk," protested Honoria. "You make sculptures out of marble and clay and things like that."

"Sometimes yes, and sometimes no," Señor Picasso said. "Even if you give most people slabs of beautiful marble and magnificent paints, they will still make junk from it. But because you children and I are great artists, we can take junk and make great art from it instead."

He rummaged around in the junk for a moment, pulled out a few objects, and showed them to the children. "What do these look like?"

"An old bicycle seat, and some bicycle handlebars," said Honoria.

Señor Picasso arranged the seat and handlebars on the ground so they looked like this:

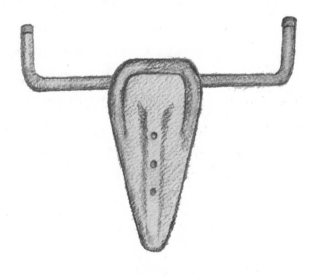

"And now?"

The children gathered around and looked down.

"It looks like a bull's head!" exclaimed Alice.

"Exactly," said Señor Picasso. "A few moments ago, these things were garbage, trash, nothing. And now—they have been made into something else completely, a work of art by a great artist. Now go find more interesting objects," he added, "and load them into the wagon."

The children ran into the junkyard and began to rummage. They carried back all sorts of things: a bent shovel, a big wicker basket, some old oil cans, a rusty pitchfork. At first, Gaston leaned against the wagon and smoked his cigar and watched them, but then even he got interested in the proceedings and started to rummage himself. As Alice dragged a dirty, crooked bicycle wheel through the yard toward the wagon, she imagined what Old Miss Pennyweather's face would look like if she saw Alice there, digging through a junkyard. The image made her stop in her tracks and laugh out loud.

When Señor Picasso felt they had enough junk, they began the journey back to Villa America. Everyone walked alongside the wagon and helped carry things so the load wouldn't be too heavy for the donkeys. When the group got to the house, they unloaded the wagon on the terrace.

Mrs. Murphy came out of the villa, her pearls swaying. She stopped in her tracks when she saw the small mountain of junk.

"Pablo," she said, and then, after a moment: "Tell me what's happening here."

"It's art, Madame," Señor Picasso told her. "Or it will be soon, anyway."

Mrs. Murphy took a deep breath and collected herself.

"Kindly bring this experiment to the back of the garden," she said. "We are having a dinner party this evening, and I'm afraid that this pile of junk—I mean, this promising pile of art materials—might get in the way."

The junk pile was now transferred to the back of the property, hidden from view by groves of lemon, olive, and fig trees. The children laid all of the objects in a long line. Señor Picasso then stalked up and down, inspecting and evaluating each one.

"Aha," he said at last, picking up a falling-apart barrel. "Here we have the beginning of something." He placed the barrel sideways on the ground. "What is this?" he asked the children.

"A busted-up old barrel," said Baoth, who was getting a little cross after all of the manual labor.

"It *was* a busted-up old barrel," said Señor Picasso. "Now it is a big, fine rib cage, belonging to a big, fine goat. Here—bring me that broomstick, please."

Alice pulled it out of the junk pile and handed it to him. The artist snapped it into four pieces over his knee. He jabbed each piece into the bottom of the barrel, and stood it up on top of the sticks. That ratty barrel was indeed being transformed into the body of a big, fine goat.

"It needs a neck," said Patrick, who rummaged in the pile and came up with a cracked metal pitcher. Señor Picasso took it and tied it to the front end of the barrel. Then he tied the broken bicycle seat to the top of the pitcher, and it became, quite convincingly, the goat's head. The children stuck tufts from the broom's bristles all over the goat, and it soon had quite a fur coat.

Mr. Murphy strolled through the gardens. He caught sight of the goat and laughed.

"What *is* that thing?" he asked.

"His name," Señor Picasso informed him, "is Gerald Goat."

"I'm very flattered," said Mr. Murphy. "Is he a well-behaved goat?"

"Not particularly," said Señor Picasso. "But he can keep up a good conversation at the dinner table."

"Hmmm—this just gave me an idea," said Mr. Murphy. "Please go inside, children, and get ready for tonight. Our dinner guests are arriving soon, and we will have a special treat waiting for them."

❧

THAT EVENING, the dinner-party guests began to arrive. Now bathed and dressed—this time in one of her fancier New York dresses—Alice sat with Honoria, Baoth, and Patrick under the silver linden tree, watching the grown-ups mingle on the terrace. The women wore silk gowns and the men wore black evening suits. Isabelle glided in and out of the house, carrying a tray shining with goblets of champagne.

Mr. Murphy sauntered out of the house, wearing a tuxedo. His hair had been slicked down with pomade, and his glinting sword dangled from his side. As he greeted each of the guests, he appeared to tell them a secret. Then he came and sat with the children.

"I have just been telling everyone," he whispered, "that we will have a special guest of honor here tonight."

"*Do* we have a special guest coming?" Honoria whispered back in surprise.

"You'll see," said Mr. Murphy, looking mysterious.

Two ladies in silky beaded dresses drifted past the children, their faces rosy with excitement.

"Who do you think it is?" said the first one to the other.

"Royalty," said the second lady. "In fact, I'm sure of it. Why keep it such a secret otherwise?"

"*Yes,*" said the first lady. "The Prince of Wales, I bet."

"Or perhaps someone from the Russian imperial family," responded the second lady, adding: "Those poor things, banished from Russia forever."

"Or both. The Murphys do know fascinating people from all around the world, of course."

Soon all of the guests were whispering to each other about the mystery guest. A few of the ladies disappeared into the house and reemerged with fresh coats of lipstick and smoothed-down hair.

Mr. Murphy stood up. He clinked the side of a champagne glass with a spoon and cleared his throat.

"Ladies and gentlemen," he announced. "Sara and I are pleased to welcome you here to Villa America this evening. And now I have the honor of introducing a special, surprise visitor. Come forth, guest of honor," he called, *ting*ing the side of his glass several more times.

The door opened a crack, and Mistigris teetered out, wearing a bow tie. One of the ladies shrieked, mistaking the monkey for a large rat.

"Oh, Mistigris—no one asked for you," Gerald told him. "Go away before I make you into a hat. And now: Could the *true* guest of honor come out, please?"

Señor Picasso bounded out of the house. Alice and the Murphy children giggled together at the sight of him. He was still wearing his tatty black-and-white-striped shirt and ragtag top hat, but had also put on a bow tie. He bowed deeply, and once again, the top hat clattered to the ground.

Giving each other disappointed looks—for Señor Picasso was already a regular Murphy visitor, and therefore hardly qualified as a "special guest of honor"—the guests clapped politely anyway.

"Oh, not *you* either, Pablo," said Mr. Murphy, exasperated. "Go inside and get the *real* guest, please."

Everyone looked hopeful yet again as Señor Picasso marched back inside.

The door slapped open and out rolled Gerald Goat, mounted on a silver bar cart. The junkyard goat too was now wearing a bow tie, and had a lit cigar stuck in its mouth. Several of the ladies gasped.

"What *is* that horrid thing?" said one.

"It appears to be a *goat,*" said her crestfallen companion. "Made from junk. I've never seen anything so ghastly."

"Is this some kind of a joke?" sniffed another guest.

"This fine goat just happens to be the latest work of Señor Picasso—who, as you all know, is widely considered one of the most innovative artists of all time," announced Mr. Murphy. "It was created on these very premises this afternoon, with some help from his four very promising young assistants."

Here the children beamed with delight. Baoth even gave a little bow with his head.

"Enjoy its company tonight," Mr. Murphy continued. "Tomorrow, it is being taken away to the Louvre Museum in Paris."

"Oh!" cried one of the ladies. "Well. In that case, I love it."

"Magnificent," cried another now-reformed guest. "It's clearly a masterpiece."

"I say," said a third guest. "Thunderously clever."

Mr. Murphy grinned at Señor Picasso.

"Pablo, please make the introductions."

Señor Picasso wheeled the smoking goat around the terrace and formally introduced it to each of the guests. As this silly scene was unfolding, Mrs. Murphy came over and sat next to Alice.

"Well, Alice—I'm not sure if this was the sort of scene your father had in mind when he sent you to stay with us," she said. "Mr. Murphy and Señor Picasso can be quite ridiculous when they get together. I will tell you this: your mother thought they were hilarious."

Across the terrace, Señor Picasso borrowed the cigar from the goat, took a puff, and then stuck it back in the goat's mouth. Everyone laughed.

"I can't even imagine, however, what your poor governess would say about all of this," Mrs. Murphy added.

Alice watched the smoking goat making the rounds. It made her feel close to her mother to see ridiculous things happening that would have made her laugh. For once, thinking about her made Alice feel warm instead of stricken.

"I don't care what Miss Pennyweather would have thought," she said boldly. "I like Señor Picasso, and I like the junkyard goat and his cigar, and, so far, I like Mr. Murphy's school. It's a lot better than Miss Penny-weather's lessons."

Mr. Murphy gave the dinner gong several satisfy-
ing *bong*s, and the grown-ups drifted into the dining
room. The children ate on the terrace. But they could
see through a window that Señor Picasso had wheeled
the goat to the head of the table, where it was given its
own place setting and glass of champagne. It did not,
apparently, touch a bite of its food and rudely smoked
its cigar right through the meal.

LATER THAT NIGHT, up in her room, Alice wrote a letter to her father.

Dear Papa,

    Do you miss me? I miss you. But so far, the
grand tour has been very interesting. Mr. Murphy
has unusual ideas about things and so does Señor
Picasso, who gave us a lesson about making art
from junkyard things. He even made his junkyard
goat smoke a cigar. The children are very nice,
and Honoria gave me a dress to play in. We went
to the beach, where Mr. Murphy pretended to kill
a seaweed monster with his sword. Everything is
delicious at Villa America. Apparently if you eat the

gooseberry jam from here, you stay young forever.
If only we had known about it before and could
have given some of it to Mama.

Love,

Alice

PS Thank you for telling Miss Pennyweather to
go back. I know you say she means well, but I'm
happy that she's gone. Now I don't feel like I'm in
trouble all the time.

PPS I am not sleepy anymore either.

PPPS Mrs. Murphy lets me walk around barefoot.
I hope that's all right.

She put the letter aside, and listened to the guests
laughing downstairs and the sound of the jazz
musicians playing. The moon shone bright on the
Mediterranean Sea outside her window as she drifted
off to sleep.

The next morning, when the children got up, Señor
Picasso had already left. Gerald Goat—now sadly
cigarless—stood on the terrace. Señor Picasso had
thoughtfully left a pile of tin cans for its breakfast.

And that afternoon, two men from the famous Louvre Museum in Paris indeed turned up to take Gerald Goat to its new home. As they prepared to put it into a crate, the children gathered to say goodbye to it.

"So long, old pal," said Baoth, slapping him on the rump.

"Have some respect," said Honoria. "This is Art, after all."

The children all gave the goat some affectionate farewell pats. The museum workers carefully wrapped him in gauze and cloth, put him into his crate, and then drove away, quite pleased with their priceless new treasure by the world's greatest living artist.

A WEEK LATER, nearly four thousand miles away in New York City, Alice's father was settling into his library armchair, ready to read and smoke his evening pipe. Mrs. Millicent, the housekeeper, brought him Alice's letter. Mr. Atherton read it, and then read it again. He folded it up, put it on the table next to him, and took some deep puffs on his pipe.

"Not bad news about Miss Alice, I hope, Mr. Atherton?" asked the housekeeper anxiously.

"Not at all," said Mr. Atherton. "Those were puffs of relief. I am glad to report, dear Mrs. Millicent, that I believe the Murphy cure is already proving a success. That wondrous family may just be bringing my little girl back to life."

Chapter Five

SIMPLE THINGS

NOW THAT IT WAS MID-JUNE, THE DAYS WERE GROW-
ing hotter. The branches of the silver linden tree on the
terrace bowed and sagged in the afternoon heat, and
then straightened out in relief each evening when the
sun went down. Mr. Murphy unrolled the long, fringed
awnings above the villa's windows, and Mrs. Murphy
left out big ceramic dishes of water on the terrace for
the children to stand in to cool their bare feet when the
tiles got too hot. Even the bees seemed lethargic, and
the sea gave off a hazy glow.

One morning, about a week after Señor Picasso
left, Alice and the Murphy children rode the donkeys
down to the beach. As usual, Alice sat behind Honoria
on one donkey, while Baoth and Patrick rode the other.

At first, Alice had been shy about holding Honoria's waist as they lurched down the hill, but now she liked it. Honoria's hair shone in the warm sun and smelled like flowers.

The girls spread a blanket out on the sand and read books from the Murphys' library, while the boys attacked the seaweed monster, which had, as usual, washed back up onto the beach during the night.

Honoria lay on her stomach, reading and lazily twirling her feet around in the air.

"Which book did you pick?" Alice asked her.

"I'm reading about Marie Antoinette," Honoria murmured.

"Who is that?"

"The last French queen," Honoria told her. "She wore lots of diamonds and very tall wigs, and gave big feasts while most of the people in France were extremely poor and didn't have anything to eat."

Baoth and Patrick flung themselves down on the blanket.

"You know what happened to her, right?" Baoth asked Alice.

"No, what?"

"They chopped off her head," he said gleefully.

"No, they didn't," said Alice, appalled. "They

couldn't have." She paused, and then added: "Who is 'they'?"

"The French people," Baoth said. "They were fed up with her being so rich and selfish when they were so poor. So they stuffed her into a guillotine—*whack! chop!*—and after that, they didn't have queens anymore."

"Baoth, don't be a ghoul," said Honoria, still studying the book. "But she does seem awfully greedy. Listen to what they served at just one single dinner at her palace in Versailles. Four soups to begin. Then something called rump of beef."

"Rump!" shrieked Baoth with glee. "She ate a rump!"

"And loin of veal on spit," read Honoria.

"Blech," said Patrick. "Who wants to eat spit?"

"That means it's *roasted* on a spit," explained Honoria scornfully, "which is like a long spike over a fire. Anyway, that was just to begin. There were sixteen main courses. Roasted rabbits and suckling pigs, quails with rose leaves, turtle doves and partridges in some kind of truffle sauce, ducklings in orange sauce, something called chicken blanquette, and—oh, this is actually quite dreadful—calves' heads with another kind of sauce."

"What about dessert?" asked Patrick, who would have gladly eaten *anything* as long as it was doused in chocolate.

"The dessert list is almost too long to read," said Honoria. "Macaroons. Candies. Puff profiteroles with cream and chocolate—"

Patrick pretended to faint in the sand.

"That table must have been a thousand feet long," said Honoria, closing the book.

"We never get to eat anything fancy," complained Baoth. "I wouldn't mind getting to try some of that stuff."

Alice didn't say anything. She personally didn't think the feast sounded that appetizing. All her life, she really hadn't cared much about food one way or another, probably because Old Miss Pennyweather had insisted on bland meals, without salt, without spice. ("Sugar is the devil," she used to tell Alice. "So is lemonade—all of that acid! And *pepper*? Horrors! Your poor little stomach.") So much of the food that Alice had eaten had sort of looked and tasted like oatmeal.

The sound of the terrace gong rang from the villa.

"That's Dow-Dow," explained Honoria to Alice. "He said there would be a new surprise waiting for us when we came home for lunch."

Alice perked up then. She had already learned that one could not accurately predict what Mr. Murphy had planned next. And she was also already learning to love that moment just before the surprise happened. Like bare feet and play clothes and pet monkeys, surprises themselves were new and wondrous to her.

❦

WHEN THE CHILDREN ARRIVED back at the house, they saw a new automobile parked in the driveway. They led the donkeys to their water troughs, and walked around to the back terrace to see who had arrived.

"Children, there you are," called Mr. Murphy, who was sitting at the table under the linden tree. "Do you remember this little fellow? Say hi to Bumby."

A sandy-haired boy, around four years old, stepped forward shyly.

"And you surely remember *this* big fellow," boomed a voice, and a man stood up from one of the benches.

"Uncle Ernest," cried the Murphy children, and ran to him. The man looked to Alice like a tall, dark tree— the sort that had thick roots and strong branches and never swayed in storms. He had tousled brown hair and a broomlike mustache.

"Alice, this is Mr. Hemingway," said Mr. Murphy, "and his son, Jack—but his nickname is Bumby. Mr. Hemingway is a famous American writer. Newly famous, but probably permanently famous."

Mr. Hemingway seemed to like this.

"He and Bumby and Mrs. Hemingway—whose name is Hadley—have come to amuse us for a few days," added Mr. Murphy. "And he has kindly agreed to be your second teacher of the summer."

Mr. Hemingway dangled Baoth from one arm and Patrick from the other.

"You're gangly but strong," he told them, swinging them from side to side. "Come on, Honoria—you're next."

Honoria swung from Mr. Hemingway's arm so hard that she almost pulled him down to the ground. He laughed and gave her a hug.

Mrs. Murphy and Mrs. Hemingway emerged from the house, fanning themselves with paper fans. To Alice, Mrs. Hemingway looked warm and friendly, with her thick, short red hair that shone like copper in the sun.

"Children, please take Bumby and go down to the

garden and pick vegetables for lunch," Mrs. Murphy told them. "Potatoes, green beans, tomatoes. And whatever else looks delicious." She handed them several wicker baskets.

The vegetable garden was a glorious tangle of vines and bushes. Butterflies and bees zigzagged above the leaves. Hummingbirds darted overhead, hovering in front of flowers. The dirt felt warm and soft under Alice's feet. Back in New York, her family had no garden—only flower boxes in the windows, which her mother had kept filled with bright red geraniums. Here, surrounded by flowers and leaves and sunshine, Alice closed her eyes and took a deep breath.

"Wake up, sleepyhead," called Baoth, and tossed a wicker basket to her. "You're on tomato duty."

Alice had never gardened before. "How do I do it?" she said.

"Just twist them until they pop off the vine and put them in the basket," said Baoth. "But only the juiciest, reddest ones. Bumby can be your helper."

Alice and Bumby ambled into the tomato patch. To Alice, Bumby seemed like a quiet, sweet boy, a wispy shadow of his father. At first, he had a hard time pulling the tomatoes off the vine, but Alice helped him. This little act made her feel like a real, bona fide Murphy sibling: assured, breezy, wise about the ways of nature. Just when she began to feel like she'd been doing this her entire life, she felt something soft and furry underneath one of the leaves, and let out a shriek.

Patrick came running and flipped the leaf over. On its underside clung a big, fat, bright green caterpillar. It acknowledged the children with a bored gaze that seemed to say, *How dare you disturb me?* Patrick plucked it off the leaf and held it in the palm of his hand.

"You can never have too many pets," he informed Alice and Bumby. "Besides Mistigris, I have a mouse, a lizard, a moth, and three stray cats who come sometimes for dinner."

"If they're *stray* cats, then they don't belong to you," called Baoth. "They don't belong to anyone."

"They do so belong to me," Patrick said defiantly. "I'm the only one who they'll let pet them, and they'll eat fish from my hand. They always run when they see *you* coming." He looked lovingly at his new caterpillar.

Honoria came over to inspect it.

"Animals love Patrick," she told Alice. "Even when

he was a tiny baby. Butterflies always landed on his cradle, and an owl kept watch over him from a branch outside his window. Dow-Dow sometimes calls him Saint Francis, the patron saint of all animals."

A short while later, everyone gathered at the table for lunch. The children fought over who got to sit next to Mr. Hemingway. Baoth, Patrick, and Bumby all squashed onto his lap at the same time, making a squirmy pyramid on top of the writer. Mistigris climbed up as well.

"Don't mush my new pet," yelled Patrick, producing the caterpillar from his front shirt pocket and placing it on the tablecloth.

"Ugh, throw that thing away," said Baoth.

"No!" said Patrick. "It's precious to me."

"It's just a regular old caterpillar," Baoth told him, getting up and raising his hand to mash it.

"Stop," said Mr. Hemingway. His voice had the same effect as the terrace gong: it reverberated across the table. Everyone froze. He picked up the contentious caterpillar.

"Look closely at this creature, children," he said. "There's nothing 'regular' about it. In fact, this little fellow is a miracle, as spectacular as the Notre-Dame Cathedral in Paris."

"That's a joke, right?" asked Baoth, still determined to smush it. Once he made up his mind to do something, that was that.

Mr. Hemingway picked up a garden tomato from a platter on the table and held the caterpillar up next to a leaf sticking out from one of the tomato tops.

"What do you notice about this tomato leaf and this creature?" he asked.

"They're exactly the same color," said Patrick.

"That's right," said Mr. Hemingway. "And what else?"

Alice forgot to be shy for a moment. She crowded in to study the caterpillar and noticed something extraordinary that she hadn't noticed in the garden.

"Why, it's sort of the same shape as a tomato leaf too," she said.

"Exactly," thundered Mr. Hemingway. "Now don't you see how wondrous this creature really is?"

The children looked at each other, unsure of what the right answer was.

"You children have your food brought to you three times a day," Mr. Hemingway told them. "But not only does this little caterpillar have to find his own food, he has to worry constantly about becoming someone *else's* meal. A hungry hawk; a beady-eyed crow. So, somehow, over thousands of generations, his species has figured out how to blend in completely with the leaves of a tomato plant. Not only does this let him get close to that big, juicy tomato and its delicious leaves for his own meals, but it helps make him almost invisible to birds and other creatures who would consider him a tasty snack. *And* almost invisible to little children eager to smush him, just because they don't understand what a marvel he really is."

Baoth studied the caterpillar.

"I suppose that is pretty remarkable," he admitted grudgingly.

The reprieved caterpillar crawled eagerly toward the tomato. Mistigris—now perched on Mr. Hemingway's shoulder—eyed the creature warily.

"How was your morning on the beach, children?" asked Mrs. Murphy, coming out of the house with a bowl of peaches.

"Good," said Honoria. "Alice and I read while the boys killed the seaweed."

"What were you reading?" asked Mr. Hemingway with great interest.

"A book about Marie Antoinette," said Honoria. "And her feasts." She told Mr. Hemingway about the elaborate feast.

"Why can't we have a feast like that, Mama?" asked Baoth. "We always eat from the garden. I want to try fancy food."

"Me too," said Patrick. "I'm tired of tomatoes and potatoes. They're boring."

Mr. Hemingway wiped his mouth, looked at Mr. Murphy, and then looked at the children.

"Murphy, this seems like the perfect time to begin *my* lesson in earnest," he said. "No pun intended."

"What's the lesson going to be about?" asked Honoria.

"We've already begun it, actually," he answered. "It will be about appreciating the simple things that surround us—and how the things that *seem* simple can actually be complicated and incredible. The lesson will be about how a caterpillar is not just a caterpillar, and how a tomato isn't just a tomato. Nor is a fish just a plain old fish."

"You mean, a fish isn't a fish isn't a fish isn't a fish?" asked Mr. Murphy.

The two men snorted and laughed. The children looked at each other in confusion.

"Ignore me, children," said Mr. Murphy. "That was a silly literary joke. Carry on, Ernest: tell us more."

"We will also learn about how the most seemingly

simple and common things can also be the most precious things in the world," Mr. Hemingway said. "Like sunshine, and rain, and dirt in the garden, and the sea."

With his fork, he speared a piece of steamed potato, smeared it with butter, and ate it with great satisfaction.

"And, on that note, how simple foods can be the most delicious," he added. "Forget about Marie Antoinette's feasts and her fancy, stuffy little indoor world."

He turned to Mr. Murphy and asked, "Is that new boat of yours up and running?"

"It is," said Mr. Murphy. "We just put her in the water. The *Picaflor* is at your service."

"Very good, Captain," said Mr. Hemingway. "We will board the *Picaflor* at sunrise and begin."

❧

IT WAS STILL DARK when the Murphys, the Hemingways, Alice, and Mistigris boarded the sailboat the next morning. Mrs. Murphy poured strong coffee from a thermos for the grown-ups. Baoth and Patrick propped themselves up against each other and swayed sleepily with the motion of the water.

Mr. Murphy cranked up the anchor. The boat glided out into the sea, wind billowing the sails. Mr. Hemingway marched up and down the deck, lining up fishing rods against the rail. He seemed so alert and excited that Alice wondered whether he'd had about a thousand cups of coffee already.

When the shore looked like a blurry line on the horizon, Mr. Murphy lowered the anchor, and the *Picaflor* bobbed gently in place. Mr. Hemingway looked at his watch.

"The sun is going to rise in . . . three . . . two . . . one . . . *now,*" he said.

The sun came over the horizon, turning the sky pink and gold. The sea shimmered.

"Now, each of you take a fishing rod," Mr. Hemingway said. "We're going to catch our lunch. And maybe even our dinner too, if one of you hooks a tuna. Those boys are as big as cows." He smiled. "I'll help you bait your hooks."

Alice stood shyly behind her fishing rod. Mr. Hemingway came toward her, carrying a small bucket from which he pulled a little fish. He held it out to Alice, but she stepped back.

"Go on, take it," he told her kindly. "It won't bite. It's going to be your bait."

Alice had never touched a live fish before, but she summoned up her courage, closed her eyes, and took the fish in her hand. It was cold and smooth and slippery. She opened one eye and looked at it. The sun had risen higher in the sky, and shone on the creature's silvery blue scales. Suddenly Alice imagined Old Miss Pennyweather being handed a fish by Mr. Hemingway, who looked as unkempt and gruff as a pirate. In Alice's mind, the governess squawked, *A sea creature—have mercy!* and then fainted and *clunk*ed down onto the deck. Alice smiled and ducked her chin into her chest.

"See, that was easy," Mr. Hemingway told her. "Now hold that fish still while I hook it for you."

He tied a glinting hook to the line on her fishing rod and jabbed it through the fish's tiny body. Alice watched with horrified fascination. Mr. Hemingway then held the rod over the edge of the deck, dangling the bait above the surface of the water, and showed Alice how to lower and reel in the line.

"Hold on tight," he told her. "And whatever happens, don't let go of the rod."

"How will I know if I've caught something?" Alice asked, gripping the rod awkwardly.

"You'll know," said Mr. Hemingway. "Just don't let go."

The sun rose higher, and the boat swayed from side to side. The children eagerly held their rods and stared into the water, willing fish to come chomp on their bait. As the minutes ticked by and no one caught anything, they started to grow restless.

"Where *are* they, Uncle Ernest?" complained Baoth. "I'm bored."

"They're out there," said Mr. Hemingway. "Underneath the surface of the water, millions of fish are swimming and going about their business. Swimming with or against currents, hunting with their families, making baby fishes. They have a whole fish universe down there, under the surface, that we know very little about. Fish cities and countries and kingdoms."

"I wish we could see all of that," Baoth said, peering down at the sea with new interest.

Even with the allure of invisible fish cities in the sea, the children's minds began to wander. Mr. Hemingway walked up and down the deck, monitoring their lines. His pant legs had been cut into shorts, and Alice noticed for the first time that his legs were covered in little red scars, as though someone had dusted him with red sprinkles. Baoth noticed it too. When Mr. Hemingway was on the far side of the boat, Baoth beckoned to Mr. Murphy.

"Dow-Dow, what are those marks on Mr. Hemingway's legs?" he asked quietly.

"Scars," Mr. Murphy told him in a low voice. "From the Great War. Mr. Hemingway drove an ambulance in Italy during the war, and he got hurt from an explosion."

"What was the Great War?" asked Baoth.

"It was a big war that happened just before you were born," explained Mr. Murphy. "With many different countries fighting each other all over the world."

"Why were they fighting?" asked Baoth.

"No one really knows now," said Mr. Murphy, and shook his head.

"Poor Mr. Hemingway," said Baoth. "I bet that hurt horribly."

"Well, it doesn't keep him from barreling through his life," said Mr. Murphy. "It would take more than a great war to keep that man from his fishing rod and his typewriter."

They were quiet again as they watched their fishing lines sway in the water. Alice thought about what Mr. Murphy had said. She had heard her father talk about the Great War once in a while, usually with one of his authors. It seemed to her that many of them liked to write about war and talk about war endlessly, as though it were a puzzle they could never figure out and never finish.

Honoria gave a shout, and called out: "Something is pulling! Something's pulling!"

There was great excitement as she and Mr. Hemingway reeled in her line. They pulled a small silver fish up above the surface of the water. Honoria shrieked with glee.

"First catch of the day," Mr. Hemingway congratulated her. "But he's just a little fellow—too little for eating—so we're going to cut him loose."

He removed the hook from the fish's mouth and threw it back into the sea.

"I have something!" cried little Patrick, but when they started to reel in his line, everyone heard a scraping noise from the deck. It turned out that he had flicked his hook backward across the deck and not into the sea at all.

"A *broom*," yelled Baoth. "Patrick caught a broom!"

It was true. Everyone laughed. Mr. Hemingway emancipated the broom, put new bait on Patrick's hook, and dropped the line into the sea. Soon everyone's lines were twitching.

"We're in a school of mackerel," said Mr. Hemingway excitedly. "Hold on to your rods!"

One after another, Honoria and Baoth and Patrick reeled in big, shiny blue-silver fish. Mr. Hemingway unhooked the fish and dropped them into a big bucket, where they thrashed and glinted in the sun. Even Bumby caught a little fish.

Only Alice hadn't caught one yet. To her surprise, tears stung her eyes—but suddenly she felt a strong tug on her line. It was so strong that her rod started to bend.

"Mr. Hemingway," she cried. "Come quickly— please!"

"Hold tight," said Mr. Hemingway, running to help her. As he grasped the rod, Alice let go, but Mr. Hemingway told her to keep holding on.

"This is your catch, not mine," he said.

The fish gave another hard tug, pulling both of them forward.

"It's a big one," exclaimed Mr. Hemingway happily, and he began to reel the fish in. Alice gripped the rod so tightly that her knuckles whitened. "I have to reel slowly," he told her, "so the line doesn't break. This fellow is a fighter."

Everyone had gathered around them now, excited to see what they would pull out of the sea. Slowly, slowly indeed, Mr. Hemingway reeled in the fish as both he and Alice gripped the rod. Alice's hands were sore, but she held on as though her life depended on it. And just when she thought she couldn't hold on for another second, Mr. Hemingway let out an excited whoop, and from the sea they pulled a swordfish, its body glinting and shining as it writhed.

"Let go, Alice!" Mr. Hemingway yelled. "Everybody stand back."

He pulled the thrashing swordfish over the side of the deck, and grabbed it by the tail with one hand and by its swordlike nose with the other. To Alice, the creature was both frightening and beautiful. Mr. Hemingway could barely hold on to it.

"Alice, congratulations!" cried Mr. Murphy. "The unicorn of the sea—and he chose *you*. He must have something to say to you."

"But animals can't talk," said Baoth, keeping his distance.

"Yes, they can," said Patrick. "They just have different languages."

Mrs. Hemingway—who had been quiet until then—suddenly spoke up.

"Maybe he has a message for all of us," she said. "Maybe he's bringing us a reminder that extraordinary things can happen at any moment—especially when we least expect them."

"Come say hello to your unicorn, Alice," said Mr. Hemingway. "And then let's say goodbye."

"We can't keep him?" cried Patrick, who was clearly trying to figure out how to add the fish to his menagerie of pets.

"Some fish are too magical and rare to eat," said Mr. Hemingway. "And too wild to keep as pets. So we're going to send this one back to his underwater kingdom."

Alice stepped cautiously forward. With a trembling hand, she touched the swordfish's smooth, wet side.

"Hello," she said to it. "Thank you for picking me." And then she added: "I love you"—without really knowing why she said it.

Mr. Hemingway carried the strong fish to the side of the boat and threw it back into the waves. A moment later, the freed fish leaped above the water's surface— and then it disappeared.

❧

THAT EVENING, with the *Picaflor* anchored safely again near the Murphys' beach, the families gathered on the sand as the sun sank toward the horizon. The women spread big blankets out across the sand, while Mr. Murphy and Mr. Hemingway built a roaring bonfire. The children gathered stones for the fire's edge and a pile of sticks to throw on top of the flames. Isabelle came down from the villa with bags of bread, vegetables, and fruit.

Mr. Hemingway gutted, scaled, and filleted the fish that they had caught, then speared the fillets onto sticks and created little spits for them over the fire. When the fish were cooked, Mr. Murphy cut up fresh lemons with his pocketknife to squeeze over them. The children roasted potatoes over the fire on long sticks and bit into tomatoes like apples. Alice had never tasted anything so delicious, not even the butter cakes in the town square.

Honoria ran down to the edge of the sea and returned with an armful of seaweed. She draped the long tendrils around everyone's necks.

"Now everyone has pearls like Mama," she said.

Mr. Hemingway speared a potato and held it out over the bonfire.

"How did you like your day at the school of simple things?" he asked the children.

"But, Uncle Ernest, you didn't give us our lesson," said Patrick. "We just went fishing—and you forgot."

"I certainly did not," Mr. Hemingway replied. "The whole day was a lesson—the best sort: the kind of lesson that you live and isn't just said in words in a classroom. I want each of you to tell me one thing you learned today."

"That a fish isn't just a fish," said Honoria. "It's a feast."

"That there's a whole hidden world in the sea," said Baoth. "And all around us, on land."

"That my caterpillar is a cathedral," added Patrick, and then, uncertainly: "Or something like that."

Alice thought about what Mr. Hemingway's lesson had meant to her. The ocean did seem more beautiful and important now at the end of this day. And the Murphys' simple fruits and vegetables seemed more delicious, and their garden like a whole new world.

She tried to decide whether the swordfish she had caught had indeed had some sort of message for her, and wondered what the fish was doing now, out there in the black nighttime sea. Did it have a family, and a home? Did it sleep at night? What did it eat? How had it learned *its* lessons about life and the world—did it have a teacher?

But before she could say out loud what she wanted

to say—that nature and its creatures and its foods were indeed starting to seem more wondrous than ever to her—Alice fell fast asleep right there on the beach: sandy, covered in seaweed, full of food, and happily exhausted.

Chapter Six

A FULL-MOON BALLET

A FEW DAYS LATER, THE HEMINGWAYS LEFT FOR Spain to watch some bullfights. Mr. Hemingway apparently loved bullfights and saw them whenever he got the chance. There had been tearful goodbyes from everyone except Honoria.

"Bullfights are cruel," she told Mr. Hemingway. "I won't talk to you until you promise not to go to them anymore."

"They're not cruel," Mr. Hemingway said. "The bull has just as much a chance of winning as the matador."

"But the bull is trapped in a ring against his will," she retorted. "And men stick him with swords and spears. That's cruel."

"Well, life can be cruel," he told her. "Think of bullfighting as another art form, one that shows off parts of life."

"No, I will *not*," Honoria said. "If I were there, I would let the bull out of the ring. And jab that matador right on his behind with his own sword."

"Ho-*nor*-ia," said Mrs. Murphy in a low, warning voice.

Mr. Hemingway smiled. "I'd pay good money to see that," he said, ruffling Honoria's hair. "Goodbye, Murphys," he called from the car as he and his family drove off, waving.

A quiet week followed. The children played on the beach each morning and lazed at the house in the afternoons. When she had first arrived at Villa America, Alice had not been used to spending so much time with other children, and often retreated to her room to read in the afternoons. But now she often read in the garden or picked berries with Honoria. One afternoon, when reading a story to Patrick, she had even fallen asleep with the little boy under the linden tree.

It continued to grow hotter each day. Even the mornings were sultry now, unless you got up before the sun rose and its heat started beating upon the beach and the house and the fruit groves.

On one especially hot morning, at breakfast, even Mistigris seemed subdued. He sat on the terrace, half-heartedly eating an apricot.

"It's like being in an oven out here," complained Patrick.

Mrs. Murphy waved a hand fan in front of her face.

"The quiet season is really starting now," she said. "Antibes will almost completely empty out for the summer. Soon it will be just us and old Mistigris here."

"I don't even want to move," Patrick said. "My clothes are already sweaty even though I just put them on."

"So take them off," Mrs. Murphy told him. "You all can go swimming after breakfast."

"Well, it's not too hot for *me,*" said Baoth, standing up. "And we'll see about quiet season," he added.

He walked over to a phonograph that stood on a little table at the edge of the terrace. His parents had given another dinner party the night before, and had forgotten to bring it inside afterward. Baoth sorted through some of Mr. Murphy's records stacked next to the table and put one on the phonograph, which he wound up with the crank on its side.

Yes sir, that's my baby,
No sir, don't mean maybe,
Yes sir, that's my baby now . . .

Alice watched appreciatively as Baoth danced to the song. Before meeting Baoth, she had never seen a boy who danced like him, with such ease and airiness. When the song was over, he took a deep bow. The children and Mrs. Murphy clapped.

Mr. Murphy came out of the house, holding a sheaf of letters.

"Alice, there is a letter for you from your father," he told her, handing her an envelope. Then he opened and studied a telegram as Mrs. Murphy poured him a cup of coffee.

"Nice news or not-nice news?" she asked. "Or somewhere in between?"

"A mix of nice and, um, interesting news," he said, looking up. "Serge has agreed to come here."

"Oh!" said Mrs. Murphy. "Well, there's the nice news. But what's the 'um, interesting' news?"

"He's going to have a dozen of his ballet dancers with him," Mr. Murphy told her.

Mrs. Murphy set down her coffee cup.

"Gerald," she said. "Where on earth are we going

to put a troupe of ballet dancers? What are they going to do—sleep on the floor of the living room and out here on the terrace?"

"Well, it does get cool at night," reasoned Mr. Murphy.

"Absolutely not," said Mrs. Murphy. "Serge's ballet dancers are the most extraordinary dancers in the world. They have to take care of their bodies. We can't have them just lying around on the hard ground, for heaven's sake. What are we going to do?"

Mr. Murphy stuffed the telegram back into its envelope.

"There's just one thing to be done," he said. "I will have to ask our friend Antoine to host them at his hotel."

"But he's already closed the hotel for the summer," Mrs. Murphy said. "It's all shuttered up."

"Well, maybe when Antoine hears that it's Serge, he'll agree to reopen it for a few days," said Mr. Murphy. "He does admire him so, and he feels terrible that Serge can never go back home to Russia again, after the revolution there. I'll drive over to the hotel today and do my best to pull on his heartstrings."

"Excuse me, please," said Alice, raising her hand a little bit.

"Yes?" said Mr. Murphy, amused by her politeness.

"Who is Serge?"

"You, Alice, are soon going to have the privilege of meeting the great Serge Diaghilev," Mr. Murphy responded. "He owns the greatest and most creative ballet company in the world, called the Ballets Russes. He also happens to be a dear friend of ours, and I asked him if he would consider becoming your next teacher of the summer. To my delight, he has accepted my request."

He handed the telegram to Mrs. Murphy, and turned to Baoth.

"This will likely interest you in particular: Mr. Diaghilev will be bringing some of his best-ever leading men," he said.

Baoth stood straight up. "What do you mean, leading men?" he asked. "Boys can be ballet dancers too? In a real performance, on a real stage?"

"Of course," Mr. Murphy responded. "Over the years, some of the Ballets Russes' more extraordinary ballet dancers have been men—and they defy gravity. You'll see."

"But Grandfather Murphy told me that boys and men don't dance in real life," Baoth said. "At least not outside ballrooms, he said."

"Don't you listen to a word that my father has ever told you," said Mr. Murphy, glowering. "He's a fusty, old-fashioned man with fusty, old-fashioned ideas. How dare he—"

He put his coffee cup down abruptly, and marched inside.

"Why is Dow-Dow so grumpy all of a sudden?" Baoth asked Mrs. Murphy.

"Well, sometimes he gets upset when he thinks about your grandfather back in New York," she explained. "It's one of the reasons we came to France in the first place. We wanted new ideas, new ways of looking at the world. Grandfather Murphy often has old-fashioned opinions about how people should behave and what they should be able to do with their lives."

To Alice, Grandfather Murphy sounded a bit like Old Miss Pennyweather, who was set in her ways and views and would likely never change. She took her letter into the library and opened it.

Dear Alice,

I was delighted to get your letter, and hear about what fun you've been having. You were brave to stay there when I called Miss Pennyweather home, and I am proud of you. Our house is dull and quiet this summer without you, but I am managing.

Please send me further news about your adventures. When Mr. Murphy wrote to me about the "teachers" he is bringing from around the world to instruct you, I was astonished and pleased. These artists are all making history with their work, if not helping to reinvent the world. Not only are they teaching us about new ways to see, they are also showing us about how much we have to learn from each other, no matter where we are born or what language we speak. Someday you children will realize how truly lucky you were to meet them.

Until then, enjoy every moment. I know that your mother would have. I wish I could be with you.

With love from,
Papa

THAT AFTERNOON, Mr. Murphy and Gaston hitched up the donkeys to the wagon and went down the hilly

Villa America driveway. The children watched as the wagon made its way along the winding cliffside road, and then disappeared into a small cliff-top grove of olive trees.

"Where is the hotel?" Alice asked Honoria.

"Do you see that building on a cliff off in the distance?" Honoria replied, pointing. Alice squinted. The heat bent the air into waves, but through the shimmer she could make out a grand marble building perched on a modest cliff over the sea.

"That's it," said Honoria. "It's called the Hotel du Cap, and it's owned by a nice Italian gentleman named Antoine, who usually closes it up during the quiet season. Dow-Dow says that we're the only ones crazy enough to stay around here in all of this summer heat."

An hour later, the wagon came tilting and creaking back down the hill.

"Once again, I have a mix of nice news and interesting news," Mr. Murphy informed the family. "The nice news is that Antoine has agreed to open the hotel for Mr. Diaghilev and the Ballets Russes dancers."

"And the interesting news?" asked Mrs. Murphy warily.

"All of his hotel workers have gone home for the summer, except for one cook and one chambermaid, who stayed on to help take care of a reclusive guest who decided to stay for the summer," replied Mr. Murphy. "So we will have to help Antoine get everything set up, and also help him run the hotel while the ballet troupe is there."

Baoth groaned and ran toward the door.

"That means *all* of us," Mr. Murphy called to him. "The troupe is supposed to arrive tomorrow, so we have to start setting up right away. Everyone get into the wagon this instant. All four young sprites, please. And you too, Sara—"

Mrs. Murphy gave Mr. Murphy a terrible, stony stare.

"Come now, my darling," he said. "It's all in the name of our children's education."

The full wagon lurched along the cliffside road once again, under a canopy of olive trees. Alice was squished between Honoria and Patrick. Even Mistigris had joined for the ride, sitting on Sara's lap and playing with her pearls.

Soon the Hotel du Cap came into view. It looked to Alice like a pale marble palace with blue shutters, all closed to discourage the sun. A sea of wilting roses surrounded the building, and tall palm trees swayed in the sea breeze.

Signor Antoine Sella, the hotel's owner—a slight, dapper man with thick salt-and-pepper hair parted down the middle and a bushy black mustache—waited for them on the front stairs. Even though it was about a million degrees out, he wore a suit, a white shirt with a starched collar, and a necktie with a pearl tiepin.

"Children, this is Signor Sella," said Mr. Murphy. "Originally of Italy."

"Buon pomeriggio," Signor Sella said as the Murphy family, Alice, and the monkey got out of the wagon. "Good afternoon. Mr. Murphy, only for you and the great Serge Diaghilev would I open my hotel in the middle of the summer. You are very wicked to interrupt my rest like this."

Mr. Murphy laughed. Signor Sella snapped his fingers in the air.

"There is not even time for a single guffaw," he said, and began assigning each of them jobs to do. To Baoth: "You will open all of the shutters covering the windows."

To Honoria and Alice: "You will be putting sheets and blankets onto the beds."

To Patrick: "You will place towels and soap in the

bathrooms, and turn on the faucets to make sure that the water is working in each. They haven't been turned on in a few weeks, you see."

To Mr. and Mrs. Murphy: "You will assist the chef in the kitchen."

"Ouch," Mr. Murphy exclaimed, rubbing his arm. Mrs. Murphy had just given him a hard pinch.

"If there's any onion chopping to be done, that will be your job," she told him, glaring.

"And what about him?" Baoth asked Signor Sella, pointing to Mistigris.

"This fine fellow will be my maître d'," Signor Sella said. "Come on, monkey—let's get you into an appropriate uniform."

Mistigris scampered up onto Signor Sella's shoulder and they went inside. To Alice, they looked like longtime best friends, reunited after a lengthy separation.

The shuttered hotel was dark and cool inside, and the sheets that Antoine heaped into Honoria's and Alice's arms smelled like fresh roses.

"Do you know how to make a hotel bed?" Honoria asked Alice as they walked into the first bedroom. "Because I don't."

"I don't either," Alice admitted. Back in New York,

her bed making had been supervised daily by Old Miss Pennyweather, who had asked Mrs. Millicent to boil the sheets each week in water and vinegar to get rid of possible germs. By comparison, these Hotel du Cap sheets seemed like soft clouds.

"Well, how hard can it be?" asked Honoria. "Let's give it a try."

The girls stretched a sheet across a bare mattress. When Alice leaned across the bed to smooth out the sheet, Honoria billowed another sheet over her and began tucking it in, accidentally sealing Alice—who squawked loudly—into the bed.

Signor Sella heard the commotion and peered into the room. Mistigris followed him.

"Honestly, Mistigris could do a better job than you two," Signor Sella told them. "Stand back and watch me," he commanded, and proceeded to make the bed with violent efficiency. When he was done, the sheets were pulled so tight that Alice wondered if anyone could ever pry them off the bed again. The girls did their best with the other beds.

Suddenly they heard the sound of motors roaring and voices cheering outside. Baoth ran down the hallway and saw the two girls standing there.

"Come quick—they're here, they're here!" he

shouted. "They're early. Signor Sella is practically having a heart attack. All of the dancers are arriving on boats behind the hotel."

The children ran out onto the back terrace just as three motorboats approached the hotel's long dock, which jutted out from the rocky cliff. Each boat held four or five people, and each person held up high above his or her head a large, brightly colored silk scarf that whipped in the wind high into the air. It was one of the most astonishing sights that Alice had ever seen: the scarves looked to her like scarlet, yellow, blue, and green flames flickering up into the sky.

Mr. and Mrs. Murphy—also standing on the terrace—cheered and clapped at the spectacle. Even a very pink-faced and distressed Signor Sella managed some applause. The boats pulled up alongside the dock, and the men tied them to the docks with rope. A dark-haired, well-dressed gentleman stepped off the first boat and bowed. A monocle glinted over his right eye.

"Gerald," he called. "Sara. Antoine."

"Serge!" yelled Mr. Murphy, and the men embraced.

"Please meet my dancers," Mr. Diaghilev said. "Ladies first. Allow me to introduce Anastasiya, Collette, Anna, Sophie, Mathilde, and Diana." Each lady stepped off her boat as her name was called. Next came the men: "And here are Michel, Anton, George, Valentin, Theodore, and Vaslav." Now standing altogether on the dock, Mr. Diaghilev's dancers looked to Alice like a flock of elegant, long-necked, gangly swans.

"Welcome, welcome," cried Mr. Murphy. "Thank you so much for coming, my old friend. You remember Honoria, Baoth, and Patrick, of course. And this is Alice Atherton, our summer guest—although she's an honorary Murphy now." Alice's face flushed with pleasure. "They will all be your students this summer."

"Enchanted," said Mr. Diaghilev, bowing slightly, "honored, and delighted. Now, something I must know right away: What is for lunch?"

"Because you are a whole day early," said Signor Sella, looking stricken, "we only have the food that we have been preparing for our sole summer guest, an American gentleman with a delicate stomach who mostly eats white rice and fish."

"So that is what we will have as well," said Mr. Diaghilev. "We will all help make this luncheon. It is the least we can do, considering that we were inconsiderately and unstylishly early."

The dancers followed Signor Sella up the cliff's

stairs and into the hotel kitchen to help prepare the feast. Honoria, Alice, Baoth, and Patrick ran around the hotel property and picked lemons and oranges from the fruit trees, which Signor Sella's cook then sliced up and baked right on top of about ten large, silvery fish. When the feast was ready, the dancers and the Murphys and Alice carried platters of food out to the terrace table.

"Shall we ask your other guest, the rice-and-fish gentleman, to join us?" Mr. Diaghilev asked Signor Sella.

"Alas, he insists on eating alone," answered Signor Sella. "That's why he comes here in the summer—because no one else is at the hotel. He is a great mystery even to us."

❧

ALICE AND THE MURPHY CHILDREN peeked shyly at the dancers as everyone ate. To Alice, they did not seem to have been put together like most other humans. The women had such long, willow-thin, but strong arms and legs, and they moved with great delicacy. The men were lean but had powerful haunches, like horses. The dancers all spoke to each other in various languages, like a musical ensemble with many different instruments.

When everyone had finished eating, Mr. Diaghilev gestured for the children to come and sit around him at the table.

"I understand that one of you is a dancer," he said. "Which one?"

Baoth looked bashfully at the ground. Honoria nudged him on the shoulder.

"It's *him*," she said. "He sings and dances all the time."

"He even dances in his sleep sometimes," Patrick piped up. "We share a bedroom and Baoth is always kicking the sheets off his bed in the night. I hardly get any sleep with all that dancing going on."

"Do you want to be a dancer?" Mr. Diaghilev asked Baoth.

"I don't know," Baoth replied. "I think so."

"Let me see you dance, then," said Mr. Diaghilev. He leaned back and called out to one of the dancers. "Valentin—may I borrow you for a moment?"

A young man stood up from the table and walked over to Mr. Diaghilev.

"This is Valentin, who is from Russia, like me," said Mr. Diaghilev. "Now, Baoth, stand next to him and do exactly what he does."

Baoth dutifully stood next to the Russian dancer, who put his feet together and circled his arms in front of him. Baoth did the same.

"Tendu," called out Mr. Diaghilev.

Valentin gently swept his left foot forward, pointed his toes straight out, and swept it back again. Baoth did the same.

"Battement frappé," instructed Mr. Diaghilev.

The Russian dancer pointed his leg straight out, then back, then to the side and back, and, finally, behind him and back to the starting position. Baoth watched him as carefully as a cat surveying a mouse, and followed his lead.

"Now plié," said Mr. Diaghilev.

Keeping his feet together and his back straight, the dancer slightly bent his knees and sank down, then rose again to a standing position. So did Baoth.

"Grand plié, please," said Mr. Diaghilev.

This time, Valentin bent his knees farther, sank much lower, and rose again slowly. Baoth bent his knees and tried to sink down too. His legs began to tremble and then—*wump*—he fell backward on his behind. Valentin laughed and helped the boy up.

"That happens to everyone at first," said Mr. Diaghilev. "Yet you have very good balance and surprising grace—especially for an American."

"Ahem," called out Mr. Murphy, who had been watching keenly from the other end of the table.

"You have not had lessons before?" Mr. Diaghilev asked Baoth.

"No, sir."

"Well, if you are a famous dancer someday, you can tell people that you had your very first lessons with Serge Diaghilev and the Ballets Russes," Mr. Diaghilev told him. "Gerald," he called up the table, "you are the first to bamboozle such a thing out of me. I never teach beginners."

"That's not fair," Honoria muttered under her breath, and then stood up. "Mr. Diaghilev," she said bravely, her face reddening. "Those will be important lessons for Baoth, and we all very much want him to have them. But will you have a lesson for the rest of us? Patrick and Alice and I aren't dancers. And this is supposed to be a summer school for us too."

Mr. Diaghilev smiled at her kindly.

"I have decided that all of us—the Ballets Russes dancers and the Murphy children alike—are going to perform a new ballet this week," he announced. "Next Saturday night is a full moon. We have one week to conjure up this ballet and practice it, and on that full-moon night we will perform it on this beautiful seaside terrace. Young Mr. Baoth here will get a solo. But I promise you there will be an important—and hopefully pleasurable—lesson in it for each of you."

Signor Sella groaned.

"A whole *week*," he said. "So much for the quiet season."

❧

THE NEXT DAY, as the Murphys and Alice were finishing breakfast back at Villa America, one of Mr. Diaghilev's dancers arrived and handed Mr. Murphy a letter written on Hotel du Cap stationery. Mr. Murphy studied it.

"It appears," he told the family, "that Mr. Diaghilev discovered a stash of Mr. Sella's Italian coffee after we left yesterday. And then he drank so much of it that he stayed up most of the night, writing our new ballet. We are to report to the hotel right after breakfast to begin working on it."

An hour later, the family materialized at the Hotel du Cap. Mr. Diaghilev met them on the front stairs. His coffee apparently still had not worn off, for he was in a state of excitement. His monocle practically trembled on his face.

"I was so inspired by the idea of the full-moon performance," he told everyone, "that I wrote a ballet about celestial bodies."

"*What* bodies?" blurted out Baoth, looking disgusted.

"*Cel-est-eee-ahl* bodies," said Mr. Diaghilev haughtily. "Planets in the sky, stars, that sort of thing. Now, line up and I will assign your roles."

Glancing at each other nervously, the children lined up.

"You, Honoria, will be Saturn, because that planet is among the biggest and because you are the eldest child," Mr. Diaghilev said, consulting a list. Honoria must have looked unconvinced, so Mr. Diaghilev told her: "Saturn also happens to be exceptionally beautiful." This information improved matters considerably.

"And you, Patrick," he continued, "will be Mercury, because you are the littlest and so quick. Alice, you shall be the moon."

"Why the moon?" asked Alice.

"Because," Mr. Diaghilev said, "the moon goes through many changes, and yet it is always calm and secure in the sky. And from what I understand," he added, "you too have been through many changes but seem quite serene, from what I've observed during our brief acquaintance."

Mrs. Murphy put a hand on Alice's shoulder. "This is true," she said. "You are a perfect moon."

Alice looked at her. "What planet would my mother have been?" she asked.

"Oh, Jupiter, certainly," Mrs. Murphy told her. "The most exciting planet, full of dramatic beauty."

"Ahem," said Mr. Diaghilev imperiously. "Attention, please. Now, Baoth—you will be Mars, because you are a fierce and fiery spirit. And you will also be our soloist, as promised. But this means that each day, you must train with us to get ready for the role—starting this instant."

He turned and called over his shoulder: "Signor Sella! Please bring me more coffee at once."

Signor Sella appeared wearily in one of the hotel windows above.

"No more coffee for you," he replied. "Ever again."

Baoth went off with Valentin to begin his lessons. Honoria, Alice, and Patrick were handed over to a young string bean of a dancer named Collette. She took them onto the back terrace, and there she handed each of them one or more silk scarves like those that the Ballets Russes dancers had held on the arrival boats.

"These scarves are the colors of your planets," she told them, the words lilting with a French accent. "Each of you will cross the terrace—our 'stage'—and pretend that you are a rising planet in the night sky. Let us begin with you, little one." She beckoned to Patrick.

"Because Mercury is the messenger planet, and is very fast," Collette told him, "you must zip across the stage several times and back, very dramatically and full of certainty. You will hold this orange scarf so it billows out behind you." Patrick ran back and forth several times, waving the scarf around in the air.

Honoria stifled a giggle. "He looks like a little rooster running around a farmyard," she said to Alice.

"And *you,* our Saturn," said Collette to Honoria, "will waltz across the stage. This planet is very serene and majestic, and you must be too." And here Collette spun in a slow, dreamy sort of way across the terrace, twirling silver scarves around her body. Honoria imitated her, looking sheepish. Collette watched her, with amusement in her eyes.

"A good start," she said. "You will improve with practice. And now—where is my moon?"

Alice stepped forward, her face red. She had never performed in any capacity before, but didn't want to disappoint Collette or the Murphys.

"As you know, the moon likes change very much," Collette explained. "Every night she puts on a new face. Sometimes her face is round and silvery, and sometimes she hides it altogether. Your dance, Alice, will show us the phases of the moon. You will glide across the stage slowly, holding a black scarf to symbolize the dark new moon. And then when you get to the middle—*poof!*—you switch it to a silver scarf to symbolize the full moon."

Alice liked the sound of all of this. Her mother had loved the moon, and sometimes she would sit in Gramercy Park on full-moon nights, watching it slowly move across the sky above the city. Alice and Collette practiced her dance several times until Collette looked satisfied.

"That was pretty easy," said Honoria to Alice confidentially as the two girls sat near the edge of the cliff afterward, eating oranges. "I wonder why it took Mr. Diaghilev all night to make that up."

"Maybe Baoth's part is harder," suggested Alice.

"Let's go spy on his lesson," said Honoria.

They tiptoed into the hotel and sneaked into a room overlooking the side lawn, where Mr. Diaghilev and Valentin were giving Baoth his lesson. The girls opened the window so they could eavesdrop on the dancers.

"Now, watch Valentin as he leaps," said Mr. Diaghilev.

Valentin ran across the lawn and gave a magnificent leap, one leg extended far out in front of him and the other leg straight out behind him. He looked like a gazelle.

"Now it is your turn," said Mr. Diaghilev. "Valentin will hold your waist while you leap in space and learn how to extend your legs." He watched carefully as the dancers went through the exercise. "That is very good. You are naturally flexible. And the more you stretch and work at it, the more flexible you will become. Now try doing the leap on your own."

Honoria and Alice watched as Baoth ran across the yard and took several leaps.

"Oh, he *is* very good, isn't he?" whispered Honoria to Alice.

"Marvelous," Alice replied, and she meant it. To her, Baoth seemed like a smaller gazelle learning to leap across the plains.

The girls watched the lesson until it was time to go back to Villa America that evening.

❧

WHILE HONORIA, PATRICK, AND ALICE only had to practice a few more times with Collette, Baoth's lessons continued every day that week. One evening, over dinner at Villa America, he almost fell asleep with his face in his dinner plate.

"I think Mr. Diaghilev is working you too hard," said Mrs. Murphy with concern. "Why don't you go take a hot bath, and have a rest."

"Ballet dancers have to work hard," Baoth told her. "If they want to be good enough for the Ballets Russes."

"Are you enjoying yourself, at least?" asked Mrs. Murphy.

"I think so," said Baoth. "It *is* hard. I like Mr. Diaghilev, but he can be very bossy. And he gets sad sometimes too. He and Valentin talk to each other in Russian, and then he seems upset and gloomy and doesn't talk again for a while."

Everyone ate quietly for a few minutes, until Baoth asked, "Dow-Dow, why can't Mr. Diaghilev ever go home to Russia?"

"Because the country had a revolution," Mr. Murphy told him. "The king and queen—called the czar and czarina—were executed, and now there is a new sort of government. There was a lot of fighting over who should rule, and it's still dangerous and volatile there. The country has changed almost completely. He doesn't feel like it's his home anymore."

"That's very sad," said Honoria.

"It is indeed," said Mr. Murphy. "While our family has chosen to live in France, we can go back to

America whenever we like. But Mr. Diaghilev felt that he had no choice, and many people like him left Russia and all of their belongings and their whole way of living behind."

Something about this felt oddly familiar to Alice, and it took her a minute to figure out what. She did not know what it was like to have to leave your home forever. But she *did* know a thing or two about having your whole life change suddenly, permanently, and against your wishes—and she certainly knew what it was like to have someone you love taken away from you. To her surprise, she began to cry.

Mrs. Murphy stood up.

"I think everybody is overtired tonight," she said, guiding Alice to the door. "We can talk more about the revolution some other time."

Mrs. Murphy escorted Alice to her room and tucked her into bed. Alice took her mother's brooch off the bedside table and tucked it under her pillow.

"I'm sorry I cried at the table," she told Mrs. Murphy.

"You don't ever need to apologize for something like that," Mrs. Murphy said, stroking Alice's hair. "The sadness that comes with losing something that's dear to you—a parent, or a home, or a country—is the sort of sadness that never completely goes away. It's also the kind of sadness that sneaks up on you once in a while, when you don't expect it. And that's all right."

She opened the window shutters overlooking the sea, which shone under the near-full moon.

"But the important thing, Alice—for you and for Mr. Diaghilev and for anyone else who has lost something or someone important—is to make new homes, and become a part of new families," she said. "If you look for life and for love in new places, you'll find it."

❧

ON SATURDAY, the day of the big performance, the full moon was so excited that it couldn't even wait until dark to rise. It popped up over the horizon in the late afternoon, as if to watch the final preparations.

Mr. Diaghilev greeted the Murphys and Alice on the hotel's back terrace. He wore a top hat and a black cape.

"You are the audience," he sternly instructed Mr. and Mrs. Murphy, ushering them to a line of chairs on the terrace. Most of the Ballets Russes dancers were seated there too. "You too," Mr. Diaghilev called out to Signor Sella. "Come here and take your seat this *instant.*"

To the dancers and the children, he barked: "Performers, please prepare."

The children stood behind a grove of trees with Collette and Valentin, who made them stretch before the dancing began.

"Remember, children: looonnng limbs—and don't rush," Collette told Honoria, Alice, and Patrick. "The planets go at their own speeds through the sky, and so do you."

At last, it was time for the performance to start. The full moon bathed the terrace in silver light. Mr. Murphy had brought over his phonograph earlier that week, so everyone could practice to music. Now Mr. Diaghilev cranked it up and placed the needle on a record. The music began.

"Ladies and gentlemen," said Mr. Diaghilev. "I present to you the world premiere of *Celestial Bodies.*" And then he called out: "Merrrrrcury!"

Patrick scrambled out onto the terrace, his silk orange scarf sailing out behind him. So excited that he immediately forgot Collette's instructions, he ping-ponged all over the terrace to the music, which featured a lot of crashing drums.

"Still looks like a rooster," Honoria whispered to Alice.

When Patrick finally finished, everyone clapped appreciatively.

"Next," called Mr. Diaghilev, putting on a quieter and dreamier song. "Mooo-ooon!"

"Go, go!" said Honoria, giving Alice a little push. Alice glided forward, holding out the black scarf in front of her, pretending to be the new moon moving across the sky. In rehearsals, she had felt a little silly doing her dance, but now, in the actual moonlight, with the audience gazing at her respectfully, she felt graceful and serious. When she got to the center of the terrace, she crouched, lowered the black scarf, and slowly raised the silver one above her head, and then rose slowly from the ground herself to symbolize the full moon rising. Then she glided to the far side of the terrace, swirling the black scarf again to symbolize the waning of the moon. Her performance ended when she leaped behind a bush at the far end of the terrace, where Collette was waiting.

"Magnificently done," Collette whispered to her. "Now—quickly!—go join the audience so you can see Honoria and Baoth."

"Saaaat-urn," called out Mr. Diaghilev, putting

on Honoria's music, which was grand and slow. When Honoria emerged onto the terrace, her characteristic confidence suddenly seemed to disappear. Her face taut with nervousness, she froze.

"Slow swirls," stage-whispered Collette from the bush. "You are graceful Saturn, powerful Saturn."

Honoria took a deep breath and began her swirling dance across the terrace. As she twirled, the silver scarves in her hands really did seem to transform into Saturn's rings, Alice thought. Honoria grew braver as the performance went on, and at the end, when everyone clapped loudly, she even ran back out onto the terrace and took a bow.

"A *curtsy,* not a bow," Collette called. Honoria curtsied and then ran off to join the audience.

At last, Baoth's big moment had arrived.

"Maaaarrrrrs," called out Mr. Diaghilev, and put on a new song, resplendent with thunderous drums. Baoth ran out into the center of the terrace, a red scarf tied around his waist. Mr. and Mrs. Murphy leaned forward.

Baoth started with tendus, and then he moved on to battement frappés. As he danced, his arms seemed weightless, and Alice saw for the first time that he was beginning to take on that swanlike movement of the

Ballets Russes dancers. Mr. and Mrs. Murphy looked at each other in astonishment. Mr. Diaghilev watched his pupil carefully, narrating the parts of the performance aloud to himself as Baoth danced.

"Tendu, now extend," he said, keenly observing. "Very good, now arch. Now spin—face forward. And now–grand finale!"

Baoth ran across the terrace and took a glorious leap—the one he had been practicing all week. Everyone gasped, including the Ballets Russes dancers. At the end of the performance, all of them stood up and shouted and clapped and whistled. Baoth bowed over and over again.

"Bravo, Baoth, bravo!" yelled Mr. Murphy. The family ran onto the terrace and embraced him.

"Dow-Dow, you were right, and Grandfather was wrong," said Baoth, his face flushed with triumph. "Men *can* be dancers. Maybe I can even be one."

"The idea that men cannot be dancers is simply absurd," sniffed Mr. Diaghilev. "Even offensive. Let me tell you this, Baoth: most people have no imagination about what is possible in this world. Signor Sella," he called, "I think that this occasion calls for champagne."

"We're too young for champagne," Honoria told him.

"Not for you, dear girl," he said. "This bottle is for me. I have worked very hard this week, and I deserve champagne."

Signor Sella brought out a bottle of champagne and a tray of beautiful, crescent-shaped Italian cookies to celebrate the premiere. As the Murphys and the children and the dancers ate and laughed, Mr. Diaghilev tapped the side of his champagne coupe with a spoon to get everyone's attention.

"Beyond giving Baoth his first real dancing instruction," he announced, "and beyond showcasing my creative genius to you, here is my lesson to *all* of you children, and perhaps to the adults here as well. Always rely on your *own* imaginations, and form your own ideas of who you should be. Pay no attention to the limited imaginations and ambitions of others."

"Do you really think that I'm good enough to be a real dancer someday, Mr. Diaghilev?" asked Baoth.

"We shall see," said Mr. Diaghilev. "You do have promise. That said, here is a less cheerful lesson from me: not everyone gets to become who he or she wants to be. Not everyone will be a star Ballets Russes dancer. But if that *is* what you want, then work as hard as you possibly can. Take lessons; put all of yourself into it. And if the Ballets Russes is still around when you're old enough to join the troupe, we will meet again and see what's possible.

"And now, everybody, please take your seats again," he exclaimed. "I have a surprise for you. You are about to witness the second half of *Celestial Bodies,* performed for you by the dancers of the Ballets Russes. We have rehearsed it in secret all week."

Mr. and Mrs. Murphy gasped again.

"Children, come sit, quickly," Mr. Murphy said. "And pay close attention. This is an extraordinary honor, one that you will never forget."

All twelve of Mr. Diaghilev's dancers took their places in a crescent-shaped line in the middle of the terrace. Bathed in moonlight, they began to dance. As they twirled and leaped, they did look to Alice like ethereal beings. Collette and Valentin did a glorious duet—a pas de deux—in which Valentin lifted Collette to the heavens over and over again. When they finished, the grown-ups had tears in their eyes as they clapped—even Signor Sella.

"That was just about the most beautiful thing I've ever seen," said Mrs. Murphy. "I can't believe that we are the only ones in the world seeing this premiere."

"Neither can I," said a voice behind them. Everyone

turned around, and there, standing in the shadows, was the hotel's mystery guest. He wore a tweed three-piece suit, despite the summer heat, and little wire spectacles perched high on the bridge on his nose.

"Hello, who's that?" said Mr. Diaghilev.

The mystery gentleman bowed slightly.

"Good evening, sir," he said to Mr. Diaghilev. "Congratulations to you and your dancers on this magnificent performance. It's a great honor to make your acquaintance. I'm John Emery, a journalist with the *New York Times*. Every summer, I come to the empty Hotel du Cap to try to finish a novel that I've been working on for eight long years. I eat alone; I write alone; I swim alone. Every day and every night are the same. Until today—

"I came out of my room to take my usual evening walk," he went on, "and accidentally happened upon this beautiful and historic performance. Thank you again. I'll never forget it."

And with that, he bowed again, and disappeared back into the hotel.

"What an odd fellow," said Mr. Murphy.

"But lovely manners, at least," commented Mrs. Murphy.

Later that night, long after the family and Alice

had gone back to Villa America and the Ballets Russes dancers were fast asleep, Signor Sella walked through the hotel, dimming lights and closing windows. As he walked past Mr. Emery's room, Signor Sella heard the *clack, clack, clack* of a Hermes portable typewriter behind the closed door. Perhaps his summer guest was making headway on his novel at last.

"Godspeed, Mr. Emery," said Signor Sella quietly, and switched off the last hallway light.

❦

ONE WEEK LATER, back in New York City, the Athertons' housekeeper, Mrs. Millicent, bustled into the dining room with Mr. Atherton's breakfast, his letters, telegrams, and newspapers. She tidied the room as Alice's father sipped coffee and read the *New York Times*.

Suddenly he sat straight up and clattered his cup down onto his saucer.

"Good heavens," he exclaimed.

"What is it, sir?" cried Mrs. Millicent.

"Mrs. Millicent, have a look at this," he told and pointed to an article in the newspaper.

BALLET IMPRESARIO SERGE DIAGHILEV DEBUTS LATEST MASTERPIECE IN SURPRISE PERFORMANCE

By John S. Emery

Antibes, France—Last night, Serge Diaghilev, founder of the world-renowned Ballets Russes dance company, premiered his latest ballet, "Celestial Bodies," in a surprise cliff-top performance at the Hotel du Cap. It was a masterpiece of choreography.

The short ballet not only starred some of the company's most celebrated principal dancers, but also featured several parts for children, played by newcomers Mr. Baoth Murphy, age 8, Miss Honoria Murphy, age 10, and Mr. Patrick Murphy, age 6, of Antibes, and Miss Alice Atherton, age 10, of New York City.

"Well, I never," exclaimed Mrs. Millicent. She and Mr. Atherton stared at the article for a while, until he folded up the paper.

"Mrs. Millicent, please send for my secretary," said Mr. Atherton. "I will need him to book a suite for me on the next transatlantic liner."

"Right away, sir," she said. "That must have been a bit of a shock, seeing Miss Alice's name in the papers like that, associated with show-business people. I imagine that you want to go and bring her back right away."

"Quite the opposite," said Mr. Atherton. "It now appears to me that the Murphy cure is exceeding even my own highest expectations. The time has come, I believe, for me to see it all for myself."

Chapter Seven

BEAUTIFUL CHARACTERS

EVERYONE WAS DOWNCAST WHEN MR. DIAGHILEV and his dancers returned to Paris. That is, everyone besides Signor Sella, who practically danced down the corridors of the Hotel du Cap.

"I do not want to see another soul until September, including you," he told Mr. Murphy. "Actually, Mistigris can come at any time. But no one else," he added, firmly closing the hotel's front doors.

A few mornings later, Mr. and Mrs. Murphy came down to the beach with the children. Mrs. Murphy brought along a big wicker basket filled with fruit and biscuits. Mr. Murphy brought with him a sheaf of unopened letters and began to read them.

"Ugh," he said, reading the first one. This was followed by, "Oh no," as he read a second one, and then, after a third one: "Damnation!"

"*Gerald,*" said Mrs. Murphy sternly. "Mind your language. What's the matter?"

"It was all going too well," he told her, stuffing the letters into the wicker basket. "I knew that it was a miracle to get Pablo, Ernest, and Serge to come here to Villa America at the drop of a hat. But now everyone else I've asked is too busy: Cole Porter, Igor Stravinsky, Coco Chanel."

"It's just as well that Chanel can't come," said Mrs. Murphy under her breath. "Beastly woman."

"But, Sara, their unholy education feels incomplete," said Mr. Murphy. "I feel like the children need at least one more teacher this summer, before Alice goes home. It all feels incomplete right now."

"Don't worry about it, my darling," Mrs. Murphy told him. "I was going to tell you this later today, but I actually made an inquiry of my own. And I'm happy to report that the children have not one but two teachers coming this weekend."

"Really?" said Baoth, who had been eavesdropping. "Who?"

"You'll see," said Mrs. Murphy. "It's going to be a surprise."

"Who could it *possibly* be?" puzzled Mr. Murphy. His eyes narrowed. "Sara, what are you up to?"

"You'll just have to wait to find out," she told him.

The children found that they were grateful for the calm week that followed; they were tired after the excitement of the Ballets Russes visit and performance. In the mornings, they swam in the sea—now a greenish-blue summer hue—and climbed the fruit trees. Mrs. Murphy and Isabelle watched them from an upstairs window one afternoon as the children read and drew and lazed under the linden tree.

"Alice is like a completely different girl now," Isabelle observed. "Not at all like when she first came here, when she was quiet in an unhappy way."

"I agree," replied Mrs. Murphy. "Maybe this is the first time she has ever been able to truly be herself. But what happens when she goes back to New York? It's all well and good to be happy and free when you are far away from home, on a blissful summer holiday. The question is how you bring happiness and freedom back with you."

THE DAYS WENT BY, and no new teachers materialized.

"Where *are* these mystery instructors of yours?"

Mr. Murphy asked Mrs. Murphy one evening as she was shucking ears of corn for dinner.

"They're late," she said, without concern. "As usual."

Just then, they heard a motor roaring up the winding driveway, and a great cacophony of horn honking. An open-topped car swung around the house and screeched up practically onto the marble terrace. A young man and a young woman both stood up in the front seats and waved.

"*Say*-ra!" called the woman. "Gerrrr-ald!"

"We're so sorry to be late, old sport," said the man to Mr. Murphy. "We accidentally drove our car into a ditch just outside Paris, so we had to leave it there and go buy this new one. Isn't she a beauty?"

Mr. Murphy went pale and turned to his wife.

"You asked Zelda and Scott Fitzgerald to come?" he whispered to her. "Have you lost your *mind*?"

"Don't worry," she told him. "I have a very specific Fitzgerald lesson planned."

"But they are, without a doubt, the *worst*-behaved people we know—in any country, and on any continent," he said quietly as the Fitzgeralds began heaving their luggage out of their back seat. "I love them dearly, but I can't think of a single thing they can teach the children. Except maybe this lesson: whatever you see Zelda and Scott Fitzgerald doing, do exactly the opposite."

"Don't be so narrow-minded, Gerald," Mrs. Murphy whispered to him. "As I've told you, I have a plan." To their guests, she called out: "Scott. Zelda. Welcome, dear friends. We have been waiting for you."

By now, Honoria, Alice, Baoth, and Patrick had gathered on the terrace.

"Children, these are Mr. and Mrs. Fitzgerald," Mrs. Murphy told them. "You met them when you were much younger, in New York."

To the Fitzgeralds, she said, "And this is our summer guest, Alice. You know—Archie Atherton's daughter."

"Ah, yes—Archie. He rejected my first book not once, not twice, but three times," replied Mr. Fitzgerald, fishing an open bottle of champagne out of the car. "Children, you're to call us Zelda and Scott. All of this Mr. and Mrs. business: it's very aging."

"Why, Say-ra," said Mrs. Fitzgerald. "They've gotten so big and beautiful."

"Yes, they're growing up so fast," said Mrs. Murphy, looking proudly at the children.

"No-o-o, I meant your peonies," said Mrs. Fitzgerald, and with that, she marched over to Mrs. Murphy's peony bushes, wrenched a few plush flowers off their stems, and began arranging them in her hair.

She and Mr. Fitzgerald plunked themselves down at the terrace table with the bottle of champagne.

"Now, come sit with us, and tell us everything about your summer," Mr. Fitzgerald said to the children. "Who else has been here?"

"Well," said Honoria. "Señor Picasso came and taught us that you can make art out of anything. He even made a goat out of junkyard things, and made it smoke a cigar, and then a museum came and took it away."

"Good old Pablo," hooted Mrs. Fitzgerald. "He's a funny little cigar-smoking goat himself. Who else?"

"Mr. Hemingway came," Baoth reported, "and taught us about fishing and nature and appreciating everything in it."

Mrs. Fitzgerald's eyes narrowed.

"Now, Zelda—not a word out of you," warned Mr. Fitzgerald. To the children: "She and Mr. Hemingway don't get along very well."

"Well, Scott—*you* practically *wrote* the book that made him famous—" she said.

"Enough," Mr. Fitzgerald told her. "And who else?"

"Mr. Diaghilev and some of his Ballets Russes dancers came," Honoria told them. "He wrote a whole ballet for us. And we all put on a performance, along with the real dancers, on the terrace of the Hotel du Cap, under a full moon."

Mr. Fitzgerald sat back and whistled.

"Now, those are some pretty top-shelf teachers," he said. "Zelda, what do *we* have to offer these fine youths?"

"Maybe how to do the foxtrot and the Charleston," she offered. "They look easy, but just *try* doing them on top of a restaurant table. It's hard, but once you get your balance—"

"I'm sure you remember this, children, but like Mr. Hemingway, Mr. Fitzgerald is a world-renowned writer from America," Mr. Murphy interrupted, and added warily: "Perhaps you'll teach the children how to write a story? Something along those lines?"

"Oh, good writing can't be taught," scoffed Mr. Fitzgerald. "You know that, old sport. But I'm sure we do have *something* we can teach these creatures."

Alice looked shyly at the new guests. Scott Fitzgerald was tidy and handsome, his pale hair parted in the middle and slicked down on both sides. Zelda Fitzgerald reminded her of a hungry cat, with her lovely green-yellow eyes and stealthy way of moving.

"Well, I can't come up with a lesson plan on an empty stomach," Mr. Fitzgerald said. "And we need more champagne—immediately."

"We're all out of champagne," Mr. Murphy told him.

"Well then, let's go to the café in town," Mr. Fitzgerald said.

Soon the Murphys, Fitzgeralds, and Alice were seated outside at the town square's only café. The rest of the tables stood empty, and the waiter—who had been dozing at the bar inside—sullenly walked out to the table to take their order.

"Just bring us one of everything on the menu," Mr. Fitzgerald instructed him.

"Oui, Monsieur," the waiter told him, and trudged back inside.

"Ladies and gentlemen," Mr. Fitzgerald announced to the Murphys and Alice. "I have momentous news. I have just, this minute, decided what our lesson will be this week. We shall instruct them in—are you ready?—the art of mischief."

"Um, no," said Mr. Murphy, his face reddening. "That most certainly will not be your lesson. Try again, Scott."

"Fine," said Mr. Fitzgerald. "We will instead do a scientific investigation of human nature. That's what writers are best at anyway."

He tore a menu into eight parts and handed a scrap of paper to each person at the table. Alice looked with surprise at Honoria, who gave her a bewildered shrug.

Then Mr. Fitzgerald bounded into the restaurant and returned with a handful of stubby pencils, which he scattered across the table.

"Time to make a list," he announced. "Our first subject of study will be our waiter. Let's see if we can figure out what makes him such a sourpuss."

"Maybe he has a stomachache," volunteered Patrick.

"Or maybe his back hurts him," said Honoria.

"Perhaps he had too much wine last night," said Baoth, "and has a headache."

Alice had her own opinion: perhaps the waiter thought that Mr. Fitzgerald was acting brash and rude, and didn't like waiting on him. But she kept this theory to herself.

"These are all excellent hypotheses," Mr. Fitzgerald told them. "But I think we need a more literal scientific investigation. So after we finish our dinner, we are going to saw that waiter in half and see what's inside him."

Patrick and Baoth giggled.

"On those sheets of paper," Mr. Fitzgerald continued, "everyone write down what you think we'll find inside that man."

"Oh, I do like this idea," said Mrs. Fitzgerald enthusiastically, reaching for a pencil. "I think we'll find at least half a dozen splintery old pencils, and a jumble of bent bottle caps."

"Oh, *yes,* certainly," said Mr. Fitzgerald, "and some moldy champagne corks. And a few coins, some dented spoons and bent forks, and—let's see—part of a toupee."

"Why would he eat a toupee?" asked Baoth incredulously.

"Well, why *wouldn't* he?" replied Mr. Fitzgerald. "That's the real question. People get up to all sorts of strange things, you know. Now, go on, children: write down your guesses."

The children looked at Mr. and Mrs. Murphy, unsure of what to do.

"Scott, stop being so childish," Mr. Murphy said, picking up all of the pieces of paper from the tabletop, bringing the exercise to an abrupt end. "Ignore everything he just said," he told the children. "That will be the main lesson of Mr. Fitzgerald's visit."

Later that night, Honoria came into Alice's room as the girls were getting ready for bed.

"Mr. Fitzgerald is very odd, isn't he?" she said to Alice. "What do you think of him?"

"I mostly thought he was funny," said Alice,

"although I was embarrassed when he was rude about the waiter."

The girls stood side by side in front of Alice's mirror, brushing their hair.

"He wouldn't really saw a waiter in half, would he?" Alice asked Honoria.

"Probably not," said Honoria. "But you never know. As Mr. Fitzgerald said, people get up to all sorts of strange things."

❧

THE MORNINGS WERE PEACEFUL that week, but only because the Fitzgeralds tended to sleep until noon each day. Once they emerged from their guest bedroom, Villa America seemed almost to vibrate with nervous excitement. Mrs. Murphy had told the children that Mr. Fitzgerald was one of the most famous young authors in America—and maybe the world—but it seemed to Alice that his true talent was, indeed, making mischief.

Every day, there was a new antic. For example, the day after the saw-the-waiter-open affair, Mr. Fitzgerald asked the children to show him the fruit orchards that surrounded Villa America.

"While you're out and about, please bring home some fruit and vegetables," Mrs. Murphy called after them.

Mr. Fitzgerald seemed enthralled at first by the tour of the small forest of lemon, orange, and fig trees, but he quickly grew bored.

"It takes so long to pick these fruits one by one," he complained. "But I have an idea. Does your father have a toolshed?"

"Sure," replied Baoth, and led the way. Mr. Fitzgerald emerged from the shed with a handsaw.

"Now things will go faster," he told the children, and began sawing away at various lemon and orange branches, which thudded to the ground, heavy with fruit.

When Mr. Murphy saw Mr. Fitzgerald and the children dragging the branches up to the house, his face grew red.

"Scott—have you absolutely lost your mind?" he yelled.

"I was teaching the children about efficiency," replied Mr. Fitzgerald. "You know—how to get your chores done faster so you have more time for creative endeavors and for amusements."

"Some of those fruit trees are decades old!" cried

Mr. Murphy. "What *is* it with you and handsaws, for the love of God?"

Mr. Fitzgerald looked crestfallen.

"I'm sorry about that, old sport," he answered, subdued now. He silently plucked the fruit off the cut branches and brought it inside to Mrs. Murphy.

A few days later, there was a new upset. Even though Signor Sella had closed the Hotel du Cap for the rest of the summer—Mr. Emery had left for the States again—the Murphy family, Alice, and the Fitzgeralds drove out to the hotel so they could sit on the back terrace and enjoy the view from the dramatic cliffs.

"This is where we gave our performance with Mr. Diaghilev," Baoth told Mr. and Mrs. Fitzgerald. "And I did a solo. Mr. Diaghilev and his dancers showed me that boys can be ballet dancers when they grow up."

"Who on earth told you that they couldn't?" asked Mrs. Fitzgerald ferociously.

"Well, um—" said Baoth, but Mrs. Fitzgerald cut him off.

"Boys can do whatever girls can do," she announced, and then she fixed her cat stare on Honoria and Alice. "And girls can do anything that boys do. And don't let anyone ever tell you otherwise. The world will want you to be beautiful little fools, but you two could fly airplanes, paint masterpieces, run countries. We just have to show men that girls are fearless too."

"How?" asked Honoria.

"Find all sorts of ways," said Mrs. Fitzgerald. "Like this, for example."

She stood up and walked to the edge of the cliff—and before anyone could say a word, she dove, fully clothed, into the sea below.

"Zelda, no!" cried Mrs. Murphy. "Oh my lord—it's so rocky down there. She'll break her neck!"

The family and Mr. Fitzgerald ran to the edge of the cliff and peered over. Alice's heart pounded anxiously. Down in the sea, thirty feet below, Mrs. Fitzgerald's face appeared above the water's surface and she waved triumphantly at them.

"You are the most reckless person I've ever met," Mr. Murphy yelled down to her angrily. He turned to Mr. Fitzgerald. "Both of you. You think you're teaching the children lessons about being strong and independent? You're not. You're teaching them to be as self-destructive as both of you. Children," he continued. "You are never, ever to do what Mrs. Fitzgerald just did. *Ever.* Do you understand?"

The children nodded, disconcerted by this rare show of temper.

"And you two," said Mr. Murphy, addressing Mr. Fitzgerald again, "are to leave Villa America at once. You're, you're—*banished.* This was a terrible idea."

"Now, look here, Murphy—" began Mr. Fitzgerald, but the look on Mr. Murphy's face stopped him from saying another word.

Back at the house, the Fitzgeralds quietly packed their bags. They left that evening.

❧

MR. MURPHY WAS IN a somber mood for the next couple of days, spending a good deal of time on the *Picaflor* and listening to records in his library.

"Mama, where did Mr. and Mrs. Fitzgerald go?" Honoria asked Mrs. Murphy over breakfast one morning.

"They rented a house nearby," she replied.

"Are we going to see them again? Maybe when Dow-Dow isn't so mad at them anymore?"

"I'm sure we will," said Mrs. Murphy calmly. "You can't keep them away. Mr. Fitzgerald is incapable of holding a grudge, although your father is. But if anyone can charm away your father's anger, it's Scott. You'll see."

Sure enough, the next morning, the family noticed that a paper scroll had been tied with a green ribbon to the front door's handle. Mrs. Murphy unrolled it and they read it together:

Dear Murphys (and Alice),
    This is my official plea to be allowed back into paradise. And I thought that the children should know that we found something extreemely rare and compelling, an object that might lead to an unforgetable adventure. (Gerald, I promise that it will be an adventure of the most wholesome, unreckless variety.)
    If you are intriggued, please meet Zelda and me on the beach at 5 o'clock this evening. Oh, and don't forget to bring shovels.
                                    Love, Scott
                                    (and Zelda)

"He really is the most atrocious speller," said Mrs. Murphy with affection. "Gerald, are you willing to give them another chance?"

Mr. Murphy took the letter and studied it.

"Charming, very charming," he said. "But we've given those weasels so many chances already. 'Bring shovels,' he says. At least he didn't ask for handsaws this time."

Mrs. Murphy laughed. "Aren't you even just a little bit curious about what they've cooked up?"

"*We* are," Baoth exclaimed. Patrick had already run off to find their beach shovels.

Mr. Murphy rolled up the scroll.

"The answer is no," he said. "They simply don't have any self-control, and therefore they cannot be trusted. Someone will get hurt, I know it."

"But, Dow-Dow—" cried Baoth.

"No," Mr. Murphy said, "and that's final."

The next morning, a new scroll was tied to the front door.

Dear Murphys (and Alice),

We are unsure whether you recieved our letter yesterday, and assume that either (1) an animal came by and ate it off the doorknob, or (2) You are all trapped underneath some heavy furniture in the house.

In any case, we will be waiting again for you on the beach at 5 o'clock this evening. Dont forget the shovels.

Love, Scott
(and Zelda)

Mr. Murphy took the scroll into the kitchen and threw it into the garbage bin.

The next morning, yet another scroll arrived:

Dear Murphys (and Alice),

If you don't meet us tonight, we shall be forced to find some other local children to take on this aventure—and they, not you, will likely become rich beyond their wildest imaginings, probably famous too. And then youll be sorry.

Therefore we do advise you to meet us on the beech at 5 o'clock this evening.

Love, Scott

(and Zelda)

PS—shovels!

"Oh, Dow-Dow—please let us go," begged Honoria.

"We won't do anything he says without your permission," added Baoth. "Please say yes."

Mr. Murphy studied the latest scroll. Then he turned to Alice.

"What do you think, Alice?" he asked. "Should we give Mr. and Mrs. Fitzgerald one last chance?"

Alice thought for a minute.

"Yes, I think we should," she answered judiciously.

"Because Mr. Fitzgerald did promise a wholesome and unreckless adventure, and because I think he and Mrs. Fitzgerald do mean well. And he knows that you're mad, so he'll probably be on his best behavior."

It was the longest speech she had ever given. Everyone stared at her for a moment, and Alice felt her cheeks grow pink. Mr. Murphy laughed then, and ruffled her hair.

"That all sounds very well reasoned," he said. "I'm glad that we have at least one sane person in the family. All right—I will agree to give one last chance to the reckless Fitzgeralds. But I'll be watching them like a hawk."

A few hours later, as the late-afternoon heat began to ebb, the family and Alice filed down to the beach. Mr. and Mrs. Fitzgerald waited for them. Mr. Fitzgerald appeared to be dressed as a pirate: he wore a striped shirt and a handkerchief around his head, and had even managed to rummage up an eye patch somewhere.

"Arrrgh," he called in a fake gravelly voice. "Zelda and I were having an evening dip in this old lagoon a few days ago, and you're never going to believe what we found bobbing past us in the water," he told the children, and handed them a dingy, corked old bottle.

"So a bit of garbage is the 'extremely rare and compelling' object you found?" scoffed Honoria.

"Look inside it, matey," Mr. Fitzgerald told her.

Honoria held the bottle while Baoth worked the cork out of its neck.

"Dow-Dow, Mama—there's a paper rolled up inside!" cried Baoth. He teased it out gently. "It's an old map of some kind."

The family and the Fitzgeralds studied it together.

"Why, it's a map of this very beach," Mrs. Murphy observed. "What are the chances of that—and what do we think is under the X at the far end, right there next to the rocks?"

"You all better get your shovels ready for some digging, and we'll find out," said Mr. Fitzgerald.

The children took the map and ran down the beach, until they got to the spot that the X seemed to mark. They started digging, and they worked so hard that soon they were covered with sand.

"I found something," Alice cried, her shovel *tink*ing against something hard. "Look—it's another bottle!"

She fished it out of the sand, and Baoth pulled out the cork.

"Look—there's another map inside," he said. "With an X on Cap Gros Beach—that rocky cove just down the way. But, Dow-Dow, we need the boat to get to it, don't we? Can you take us on the boat?"

Alice's heart pounded with excitement. Even Mr. Murphy had stopped glowering at the Fitzgeralds and seemed intrigued. Soon they all were aboard the *Picaflor,* sailing along the rocky coast of Antibes, past magnificent coves and lagoons filled with pale blue-and-green water. The children inspected the new map.

"It looks very old, doesn't it?" said Baoth.

"Probably four hundred years old—at least," said Patrick, looking proud. "Just imagine: it was in the beach all that time, with people sitting on top of it, and crabs walking a few feet over it, and seagulls flying above it. And *we* were the ones who got to discover it. Isn't it amazing that Mr. Fitzgerald just happened to find the first bottle, too?"

Mr. Fitzgerald attempted a humble look, which appeared most unnatural.

"Yes, it was just stunningly good luck, wasn't it?" he said.

Soon the boat approached a rock-ringed lagoon, with a sandy beach on the far side.

"We'll have to anchor out here and swim in," said Mr. Murphy. A few hours earlier, he would have been happy never to see the Fitzgeralds again, and now he grabbed a shovel and leaped over the side of the boat.

Baoth wedged the new map back into the bottle, corked it up, and jumped over the side of the boat too. The other children, clinging to their shovels, followed him. The water was shallow and warm, like a bath—not at all like the icy Atlantic, where Alice had learned to swim.

"The *X* should be right around here," said Honoria, running to the far end of the beach. The children began digging like maniacs again. This time, Patrick hit something hard with his shovel.

"Look," he cried. "It's *another* bottle." He wrestled the cork out of the top: yet another map was curled up inside.

"Let me see that," said Honoria, plucking it out of Patrick's hands. "Look, there's a dotted red line that leads us off the beach and into the little grove of olive trees just over there—and there's another *X* in the middle of it. Dow-Dow, can we go? Please?"

"How many more of these buried bottles are there, Scott?" asked Mr. Murphy.

"How am I supposed to know?" Mr. Fitzgerald replied. "We're passengers on this adventure, just like the rest of you."

The children led the way up over a low rocky cliff and into a pretty olive grove. They consulted the new map.

"I think that the *X* is right over there," said Honoria,

pointing to a sandy mound at the foot of an olive tree. The children went to work. The sand was mixed with soil, and it was harder digging this time.

"I've hit something," yelled Baoth. "And it's not a bottle. It feels more like some sort of box."

Soon they uncovered the edges of the top of a small wooden chest.

"Dow-Dow, Mr. Fitzgerald, can you help us get this?" cried Honoria. "It's too heavy for us to lift."

The men dug around the walls of the chest and heaved it out of the ground.

"It's a treasure chest!" shrieked Patrick. "I know it!" The children all leaped up and down and screamed with excitement.

"Shall we open it, children?" asked Mr. Fitzgerald.

"Yes!" they all yelled in unison.

The rusty old lock on the front refused to give way, so Mr. Fitzgerald banged on it with a shovel until it crumbled off. Then he creaked the top of the trunk open, and the children gasped. Nestled inside was a cornucopia of ancient wonders. The children pulled them out one after another and laid them on the ground: two brass compasses, three pocket watches, several broken spyglasses and opera glasses, a gold-handled walking stick, a silver monocle, a cuckoo clock, four-teen mismatched silver spoons, a hat with a broken ostrich feather jutting from the brim, and a velvet bag of dully glittering jewels.

"I can't believe it," Honoria kept saying, over and over again.

"And all of this because you found the first bottle," cried Patrick, running up to Mr. Fitzgerald and hugging him.

Alice stood in a state of joyous disbelief. She couldn't even talk. Mrs. Murphy came and stood next to her.

"Isn't this just extraordinary?" she said. "I'll trade you a penny for your thoughts."

Alice was thinking about so many things at once that she didn't know where to start. First, she was thinking that she had never seen spyglasses before, and how marvelous they were (although these were a bit cloudy when you peered through them). And second, she was marveling at how pretty the jewels were. Third, she was wondering who the owner of all these things had been, and why he or she had buried it, and why Alice and the Murphy children had been chosen by fate to find it.

Mrs. Murphy was still watching her kindly, waiting for her answer. Alice gave it her best try.

"I *think* this is what I'm thinking," she said. "That I can't believe that this gets to be my life."

Mrs. Fitzgerald overheard Alice's answer. She picked through the jewelry spread out on the sand, and found a lovely old brooch in the shape of a floral bouquet. Blue jewels glimmered as the flowers. She brought it over and handed it to Alice.

"You should have this bluebells brooch," she told her. "It goes with the sweet lilies-of-the-valley pin that I've seen you wear. It'll always remind you of your summer adventures in France."

Alice looked at the brooch. It was as lovely as her mother's brooch, and she was glad to have this souvenir. But the gift also reminded her of something that she had been working hard to forget: that summer was indeed almost over, that her grand tour with the Murphys would be coming to an end, that she would soon be returning to New York City and would be far away from all of this happiness.

Patrick gave her a little shove, interrupting her gloomy thoughts.

"Alice, come *look* at all of the loot," he said. "We're rich, and once the newspapers find out about this, we'll be famous, too."

"This is the most exciting thing," Baoth announced, "that has ever happened in the history of mankind."

Mr. Murphy walked over to Mr. Fitzgerald and put his hand on Scott's shoulder.

"Thank you, my friend," he said.

At that moment, the children saw that Mr. Murphy had indeed been charmed out of his grudge, and that the Fitzgeralds had been forgiven and admitted back into paradise.

❧

LATER THAT EVENING, back at Villa America, Mr. Murphy carried Patrick—who was fast asleep—upstairs to bed. But the three older children—still so excited that sleep seemed impossible—gathered in Honoria's room, where they spread the treasure out across the floor and took an inventory.

"Who do you suppose it all belonged to?" asked Honoria.

"Maybe that pirate Blackbeard," suggested Baoth.

"No, he was in America, not France," Honoria told him.

"Maybe it was some local French pirate, then," Baoth said. "Who was on the run and buried this treasure because he was worried about getting captured and put in the clink."

"Let's go ask Dow-Dow what he thinks," said Honoria.

Mr. and Mrs. Murphy were sitting under the linden

tree with Mr. and Mrs. Fitzgerald. Mistigris dangled from Mrs. Fitzgerald's forearm, like a luxurious piece of jewelry.

The children were just about to strut through the terrace door when they heard Mrs. Murphy say: "Where on earth did you find all of those treasures?"

"In an old antiques store on the edge of town," Mr. Fitzgerald told her. "I could have filled several chests."

Honoria gasped and grabbed Alice's hand. Tears were filling her eyes.

"It must have been a monstrous amount of work, burying those bottles and the chest, though," said Mr. Murphy. "I'm amazed that you two had it in you."

"Oh, *we* didn't bury it, old sport," replied Mr. Fitzgerald.

"Oh, heavens no," said Mrs. Fitzgerald, now dangling Mistigris from her other arm.

"No, we hired a few boys in town to help us," Mr. Fitzgerald said.

"I *knew* it was too good to be true," hissed Baoth to Honoria and Alice.

The adults' conversation on the terrace stopped abruptly.

"They heard us," whispered Honoria. "Run!"

They scampered back upstairs to Honoria's room

and closed the door. A minute later, they heard foot-steps approaching.

"Hide!" Honoria told Alice and Baoth. They plunged under her bed. The bedroom door opened, and Mr. and Mrs. Murphy entered the room.

"Come out, come out, wherever you are," said Mr. Murphy.

"And come and sit with me, please," Mrs. Murphy said, arranging herself on the edge of Honoria's bed.

The children emerged. Alice saw then that Baoth had been crying too.

"I know that you overheard our conversation with the Fitzgeralds," Mrs. Murphy told them. "And while I am sorry that you are disappointed by what you learned, I am also glad—for once—that you eavesdropped. Be-cause this gives me the perfect opportunity to tell you all—together as a family—why I invited the Fitzger-alds here in the first place. And about what lesson I thought they could give to all of us."

"What lesson—to bamboozle children and then dash their dreams?" said Honoria bitterly.

"Do you really think that's what they did?" asked Mrs. Murphy calmly. "Or rather, did they create a magi-cal adventure for you children that you'll still remember and talk about when you're old ladies and old men?"

Neither Baoth nor Honoria said anything.

"Well?" asked Mrs. Murphy.

Alice held up her hand.

"I think they gave us an adventure," she said quietly. "As a present."

Mrs. Murphy gathered Alice to her side.

"We have had several geniuses here at Villa America this summer, teaching you different ways to be creative," she explained. "I likely could have convinced Mr. Fitzgerald to give you writing lessons, or something along those lines. It would have been in perfect keeping with the other lessons this summer. But I didn't. I asked Scott and Zelda here precisely for the reasons that made your father so worried about them being here and teaching you."

Mr. Murphy looked at his wife, baffled.

"Go on," he said.

"Scott and Zelda can indeed be reckless. They can be rude, and they can be self-destructive. They're famous around the world for that kind of behavior. But one of the reasons they will always, but *always,* be welcome in our home is because of the part of them that you saw today: the sweetness, the tenderness, the devoted imaginativeness. No one is more loyal.

"I am not good with words, like some of our

guests," she went on. "But I'll try to explain my lesson. Actually, there are two of them. Firstly, to urge each of you to learn how to distinguish behavior from character. Scott and Zelda can behave badly, but inside, they have beautiful characters.

"Secondly"—and here Mrs. Murphy looked meaningfully at Mr. Murphy—"I knew they'd give us a lesson about the importance of giving people second chances. Or third chances. Especially when you *know* they have beautiful characters. Because none of us are perfect, and we will all, one day, need someone to have the magnanimity to forgive us for something we have done. Does this make sense?"

Honoria and Baoth nodded, less tearful now, and they snuggled to their mother as well. She wrapped her arms around the three children, and they were quiet for a moment.

Then Baoth sat up and looked at all of the treasure.

"Mama?" he said.

"Yes, darling?" she replied.

"I don't think we should tell Patrick that the treasure isn't from a real pirate after all," Baoth told her. "Your lessons are pretty good, but maybe he can learn them some other way when he's older."

Mr. and Mrs. Murphy laughed.

"I think we can agree to that," said Mr. Murphy. "As far as Patrick is concerned, Blackbeard himself came all the way across the Atlantic to Antibes to bury this treasure." Then he added with a wink, "We'll send telegrams to the relevant museums and newspapers tomorrow to report our historic find."

Chapter Eight

BUTTER CAKES AND MUD PIES

"DOW-DOW, MAMA, WE'RE BORED," ANNOUNCED BAOTH one morning, about a week later. "Can Gaston take us into town?"

"Nothing there will be open until September," said Mr. Murphy. "Except maybe the local dentist, and I'm assuming you're not in a hurry to visit him."

"Maybe Madame Claudette's patisserie will be open," Honoria pressed. "She never closes. And we can bring home some butter cakes. I know, Dow-Dow, how much you like them with your morning coffee." She looked slyly at her father.

"Mmmm," said Mr. Murphy. "They are indeed heavenly. The crispy, sugary top, and that soft, buttery inside." He closed his eyes, clearly thinking about their taste. "Mmmm," he said again, and then he called, "Gaston! Please hitch up the wagon. The children have an urgent errand to run in town."

It was now the middle of August. The Fitzgeralds had left for Paris several days earlier. Villa America— and the whole region, for that matter—had just started to recover from their visit. In the wagon, the children fanned themselves with dried palm fronds that Mr. Murphy had trimmed into small hand fans.

When the children ambled into the town square, they found that Mr. Murphy had been right: everything was closed. The café where Mr. Fitzgerald had threatened to saw open the waiter had shuttered its windows, and its awning had been rolled back, which reminded Alice of a turtle that had retracted its head back into its shell.

A sign that read *Fermé Jusqu'en Septembre*— closed until September—had been nailed to the door of the foot-smelling moving-picture theater.

But the biggest disappointment of all: Madame Claudette's patisserie was also very much fermé. The front door was locked, and inside, cheerful red plaid curtains had been drawn across the front window.

"Ohhh nooo," wailed Patrick.

"Let's knock anyway," said Honoria. "Maybe she's in there and has a few spare cakes."

"You do it," Baoth told her.

"No, you," she replied. "Madame Claudette can't resist you. Everyone knows that."

The flattery worked. Baoth knocked importantly on the front door. No answer. The children went around to the back door and tried their luck there.

After a minute, Madame Claudette opened the back door, looking disgruntled. To Alice's surprise, the baker was wearing a bathrobe and smoking a cigar. However, her face softened when she saw Baoth standing there.

"Allo, little Monsieur Astaire," she said to him. "And allo to you other children too."

"Madame Claudette, you simply must help us," said Baoth, looking as stricken as possible. "Dow-Dow is on his deathbed. The only thing—the *only* thing—that will bring him back to full health is some of your butter cakes. That's what his doctor said."

"Baoth Murphy," hissed Honoria under her breath.

"Is that so," said Madame Claudette. "My butter cakes are the only medicine in the world for your beloved papa?"

"I'm afraid so," Baoth said. "Can you help us? Please? We would miss him so much. We're not ready to be fatherless."

Madame Claudette took a puff on her cigar and

looked at him sternly, but a smile began to quiver on the corners of her mouth.

"You poor things," she said. "Lucky for you that I happen to have some lifesaving butter and flour and sugar in my kitchen. Come back in one hour."

"You're completely shameless," Honoria told Baoth as the children walked back to the town square.

"So what?" replied Baoth. "She loves my fibs. And I love telling them. So we all win in the end."

The children sat at the edge of the fountain and dipped their feet it. Several coins glimmered in the murk at the bottom: wishes made earlier that summer. Alice wondered which one was hers, and if her welcome wish had any chance of coming true. Nearby, propped up against a tree, Gaston snoozed with his mouth wide open.

"Where do you think we'll be going to school this year?" Baoth asked Honoria.

"I heard Mama saying to Mrs. Fitzgerald that we'll be closing up Villa America for the fall and winter, and moving back up to our apartment in Paris," she said. "So probably to the American school there. I wish you could come with us, Alice."

Alice swirled her bare feet in the fountain. "Me too," she told them.

"Where are you going to school this fall?" Honoria

asked her. "Do you think you'll have to get that dreadful governess back? Old Mrs. Peahen?"

"Old Miss Pennyweather," Alice said gloomily. "I hope not. To be honest, I don't know what's going to happen. Your parents haven't told me yet who's going to bring me back to New York, or when, and I haven't had a new letter from my father about school or a governess or anything."

"Well, let's write to him this afternoon," said Patrick. "And say that you're going to stay with us, and that's final. But I don't write very well yet, so I'll just tell you what to say, and you can write it."

Alice smiled and put her arm around the boy. He really did feel like a little brother now.

When Gaston and the children returned to Villa America with the precious butter cakes, it was still only eleven o'clock. Yet a thermometer in the garden already read ninety degrees.

"It's too hot now for the beach," complained Honoria. "But there's so much day left to fill."

"I have an idea," said Baoth. "Go get your shovels and meet me near the vegetable garden."

A few minutes later, they gathered at the vegetable garden, now a jungle filled with hundreds of heavy tomatoes and towering corn plants.

"Now, look at this nice big dirt patch," Baoth told

Honoria, Alice, and Patrick, pointing to the back of the garden plot. "I just finished reading a book about animals that live on the African plains. When it gets terribly hot there, the animals head to lakes and huge dirty puddles, and absolutely cover themselves in mud. The mud keeps them cool and also protects their skin. Let's make our own mud pit."

Everyone instinctively looked at Honoria, the eldest in the group and therefore the closest thing to an adult who could shut this outrageous idea down.

"That sounds absolutely disgusting," she said.

Baoth looked crushed.

"But divine at the same time," Honoria added, grinning. "Let's do it."

The children leaped into the bare dirt patch and began digging a long, shallow pit. Then they took wooden watering buckets from the garden, filled them at a fountain at the end of the property, and dumped the water into the pit. Patrick's job was to push dirt back into the sopping mess to make a thicker mud.

"On the count of three, let's all leap in," shouted Baoth. "One, two—"

"I can't," cried Alice squeamishly.

"Three," yelled Baoth, and all three Murphy children picked Alice up and threw her into the mud. Then they leaped into the bog themselves.

Alice stood up in the mud and gave a happy scream at the top of her lungs. She suddenly realized that it was the first time in her life that she had ever screamed. And then she realized that it felt heavenly to scream, and she did it again. Then she let herself fall backward into the muck, and that felt heavenly too. The mud was everywhere: streaming down her hair and face, caked on her arms and legs. She picked up a handful of mud and flung it at Baoth, who shrieked with delight.

"I'm a baby elephant, I'm a baby elephant," cried Patrick, crawling around on his knees and swinging his left arm like an elephant trunk.

Now covered in mud from the crown of her head to her toes, Honoria sat at the edge of the pit and announced, "Hullo, I'm Queen Victoria, and I'm serving tea. Would anyone like some milk in their tea?"

"I would," said Baoth, at which point Honoria picked up a handful of mud, flung it at him, and said, "Here's your milk," and the children all howled with laughter.

"And here's your sugar," shrieked Alice, and as hard as she could, she threw a handful of mud at Honoria.

Except the mud did not hit Honoria.

None of the children had noticed that Mr. Murphy had just arrived at their mud pit with a new, bespectacled visitor, who was, rather than Honoria, the unfortunate recipient of this handful of mud.

"Oof!" the man cried as the mud splattered across his crisp white shirt and linen suit jacket.

Alice stood frozen in horror. Then she realized who the man was.

"Papa!" she exclaimed.

She leaped out of the mud pit, ran to him, and threw her arms around him.

"Welcome to Villa America, Archie," said Mr. Murphy, handing Mr. Atherton his handkerchief.

❧

THE SUNSET WAS ESPECIALLY beautiful that night: lines of shocking pinks and bright yellows sliced across the sky. Soon these colors faded and mellowed into a deep cerulean blue. Stars began to appear in the darkening sky.

"This is indeed a magical place," said a now mud-free Mr. Atherton to Mr. and Mrs. Murphy as they sipped wine on the terrace.

"Thank you for that," said Mr. Murphy. "We didn't

want Villa America to be just a house, but a whole world, a new way of living. And we wanted it to be a place where the children's imaginations could run wild."

"Oh, the children are definitely running wild," said Mr. Atherton, amused. "My daughter among them, no less. I'd say that the Murphy cure has worked beyond my highest hopes. She's always been such a subdued child, even before Evelyn died. And now I can see how much of Evelyn's life and spirit she really has in her."

The terrace door opened and the children emerged from the house in dinner clothes. Getting all of the mud off them had required quite a bit of chiseling, soaking, and scrubbing; the upstairs bathtubs were still being decaked.

For Alice, it seemed strange to see her father sitting there on the Murphys' terrace, rather than in his library in New York. She stood shyly by the door for a moment and then walked over and sat down next to him.

"All right, come here, you terrible beasts," said Mr. Murphy. "Now that you've been deloused, come tell Mr. Atherton about your summer and everything that you've learned."

Honoria, Baoth, and Patrick plunked down at the table and, in between mouthfuls of cheese and grapes, recounted the highlights of the summer for Mr. Atherton. Alice listened quietly, reliving each moment in her mind. She felt strangely trapped between her New York self and her Villa America self, and didn't know how to act.

"Patrick caught a *broom* on our fishing voyage with Mr. Hemingway," reported Baoth.

"Baoth danced a solo that was taught to him by Mr. Diaghilev," said Honoria. "And Baoth also sneaked a puff of the cigar that Señor Picasso stuck in the mouth of the junkyard goat sculpture that we made with him."

"Tattletale," yelled Baoth.

"Mrs. Fitzgerald leaped off a cliff," cried Patrick. "But she didn't break her neck, which was good. And Mr. Fitzgerald was going to teach us how to saw open a waiter, but Dow-Dow stopped him."

Amid all of this, Mr. Atherton squinted and tried to keep track, and said things like "Oh, really!" and "Marvelous!" and "Is that so." When there was a lull in the cacophony, he turned to Mr. and Mrs. Murphy.

"This was a very international affair," he told them. "Teachers from different parts of the world. Truly a grand tour."

"Well, we think—and I know you'll agree with us, Archie—that it's terribly important for these children to have a broad worldview," said Mr. Murphy. "And to learn from an early age that no matter where we come from, or what language we speak, or what we look like, we are all humans with a great deal in common—and so much to teach each other."

"Why, that's *exactly* what I told Alice," said Mr. Atherton. "Sadly, that's a lesson that needs to be taught over and over again. Look at this century we live in. Only a quarter into it, we've already had revolutions and a great war that ricocheted around the world."

The grown-ups looked at the children.

"This generation will know better," said Mrs. Murphy softly, looking with love at each of them.

"Baoth just sneaked a sip of champagne," reported Patrick gleefully.

"You're a tattletale too," Baoth said, chasing his brother across the terrace.

Mr. Atherton turned to his daughter. "What was your favorite part of the summer, little goose?" he asked her.

Alice suddenly knew that she was going to cry in front of everyone.

"All of it," she said, and burst into tears.

Honoria came and sat next to Alice and put her arms around her, and everyone was quiet for a moment while Alice had her cry. It didn't last long, and she was embarrassed afterward as she dabbed her eyes with a napkin.

"Alice, look—it's you!" cried Patrick, pointing at the sky.

An enormous, beautiful full moon—the first since the Ballets Russes performance—had risen above the villa. Behind it glittered thousands of sharp white stars. Alice smiled.

"Let's take a walk together," said Mr. Atherton, standing up and offering his arm to Alice. "Just the two of us. Would you show me the magnificent Villa America gardens in all of this moonlight? That seems to me," he said as Alice linked her arm through his, "like a once-in-a-lifetime experience."

❦

AS THEY WALKED AMONG the olive and fruit trees, Alice began to tell Mr. Atherton about all of the things that had happened there. He laughed out loud when she told him that a lemon had thumped Old Miss Pennyweather right between the eyes when they had first arrived in Gaston's wagon.

"I would have paid good money to see that," he said.

"Wait—did you not like Old Miss Pennyweather either?" Alice asked incredulously.

"Not particularly," Mr. Atherton replied. "She was very good with you when you were a baby—and your mother and I didn't know a *thing* about raising children. Not a thing. But as you got older, I worried that she was too strict and, well . . . dreary. Then, after your mother died, I thought that I needed her more than ever."

They were standing in a lemon grove now, overlooking the nighttime sea, which glistened like silver under the moon.

"Let's sit here for a minute," said Mr. Atherton, "and take in this beautiful view."

They sat side by side, and watched the waves gently lapping at the beach far below.

"Papa," asked Alice hesitantly. "Were you mad that I was so muddy when you first got here?"

"Well, Old Miss Pennyweather certainly would have been horrified," he replied, and looked at Alice sternly. Alice ducked her chin and waited to be reprimanded. But instead, Mr. Atherton smiled and chuckled to himself.

"I, on the other hand," he said, "was never so happy as when I saw you at that moment."

He noticed then that Alice was wearing her two brooches: her mother's lilies-of-the-valley brooch and the new bluebells one from the beach treasure box.

"Alice, we have been through a terrible time," he told her. "We will miss your mother for the rest of our lives. But we have each other, and I think that this summer has given us clues about how we can be happy again. Not just here, but in New York, and wherever we go after that."

"Are we going back to New York soon?" Alice asked him.

"Yes, little goose—at the end of this week," he said.

Alice felt tears coming again. "Do we have to have Old Miss Pennyweather as my governess again?"

"No," he assured her. "You'll be pleased to hear that she has started a new job with a family that is much like ours was. The parents are young and have no idea what they're doing, and Miss Pennyweather will be greatly needed and appreciated there. And anyway, it's time that you go to school so you can be around other children. Mr. Murphy told me about a school run by a very creative gentleman—a good friend of his— right near our neighborhood."

"Well, if it's a friend of Mr. Murphy's, they probably teach good lessons there," conceded Alice.

Mr. Atherton gathered Alice to his side.

"I loved your mother with all of my heart," he told her. "And just like you, I was heartbroken when she died. But seeing you brought back to life in this magical place has brought me back to life too."

Suddenly the dread that Alice felt about going back to New York began to lift. Perhaps it *was* possible to have a new sort of life there, to take some of Villa America and its lessons and wonders back with her after all.

"Okay, Papa," she said after a minute. "We can go home. But I have a very important question."

"Yes, little goose?" said her father.

"How many of Madame Claudette's butter cakes can we bring back with us?"

"For those," said Mr. Atherton, "we'll buy an extra travel trunk if we need to."

Afterword

THE HISTORICAL PEOPLE IN *ALICE ATHERTON'S GRAND TOUR*

While Alice Atherton, her family, members of her family's household, and several other characters in this book are fictional, other primary characters are based on real people (and real animals, for that matter: the Murphys owned a monkey named Mistigris). The Murphys were indeed close friends of Ernest Hemingway, F. Scott and Zelda Fitzgerald, and Pablo Picasso. They even painted sets for Serge Diaghilev's famous ballets in Paris.

The adventures of these luminaries in *Alice Atherton's Grand Tour* have all been largely invented or fictionalized, but following are brief overviews of their real lives and accomplishments.

PABLO PICASSO

Pablo Picasso—born in Málaga, Spain, in 1881—began creating art in his childhood and had his first exhibition when he was only thirteen years old. A pioneer of modern art, he helped invent an art movement called cubism and became one of the most important artists of the twentieth century. Never content to limit himself to one medium, he painted, sculpted, drew, made prints, designed stage sets, and created ceramics, and often reinvented each of those art forms with his creative approaches. Picasso ultimately had four children of his own. He died in 1973.

ERNEST HEMINGWAY

Born in Oak Park, Illinois, in 1899, Ernest Hemingway wanted to be a great writer from an early age. He became a world-famous and bestselling author in 1926, when he released his first novel, *The Sun Also Rises.* He later won the Nobel Prize for Literature, following the publication of his novella *The Old Man and the Sea,* and is still considered one of America's most influential writers. His marriage to Hadley Hemingway failed, and he would marry three more times and have two more children in addition to Jack "Bumby" Hemingway. He died in 1961.

SERGE DIAGHILEV

Like Alice Atherton, Serge Diaghilev lost his mother early in his life: she died shortly after giving birth to him in Novgorod, Russia, in 1872. His father, a major general, remarried two years later, and Diaghilev's stepmother saw the child's artistic promise and encouraged him. As a young man, Diaghilev knew that he wanted to be a patron of the arts, including ballet, opera, and literature. In 1906, he left Russia for Paris, and in 1909 he founded the Ballets Russes, which helped reinvent ballet as an art form. Diaghilev became especially renowned for three of his early ballets: *The Firebird, Petrushka,* and *The Rite of Spring.* After the 1917 Russian Revolution, Diaghilev never returned to the country of his birth, and he died while on holiday in Venice, Italy, in 1929.

F. SCOTT AND ZELDA FITZGERALD

Born in St. Paul, Minnesota, in 1896, Francis Scott
Fitzgerald also became an internationally known author
and voice of the Jazz Age when he was still a young
man. His first novel, *This Side of Paradise,* was published when he was just twenty-three years old and
earned him much acclaim and fanfare. His 1925 novel,
The Great Gatsby, is still considered one of the greatest
American novels ever written. In 1920, Fitzgerald married Zelda Sayre (born in 1900), and the couple became
among the most celebrated figures of the Jazz Age.
They had one daughter, Frances (nicknamed Scottie). In
1934, Fitzgerald published *Tender Is the Night*—a novel
partly inspired by his longtime friends Sara and Gerald
Murphy. He died in 1940; Zelda died eight years later.

SARA AND GERALD MURPHY AND THEIR CHILDREN, HONORIA, BAOTH, AND PATRICK

Both Gerald Murphy (b. 1888) and Sara Murphy (b. 1883) came from wealthy American families: Gerald's family owned a leather-goods company in Boston, and Sara's father owned an ink and varnish company in Cincinnati. Gerald and Sara met in New York and married in 1915, and they had three children: Honoria, Baoth, and Patrick. In 1921, the family moved to Paris, where Gerald helped create stage sets and also made paintings, some of which are now in museums.

He and Sara became friends with some of the greatest creative figures in Paris and of the twentieth century, including Picasso, Hemingway, the Fitzgeralds, songwriter Cole Porter, composer Igor Stravinsky, writer Dorothy Parker, and artist Fernand Léger.

The Murphy family moved into Villa America in Antibes in 1924, but eventually returned to America in 1933. Sadly, Baoth and Patrick both died young: Baoth in 1935 of meningitis at age sixteen, and Patrick in 1937 of tuberculosis, also at age sixteen. Honoria, however, lived to be eighty-one years old, and wrote a book about her parents and their family's life at Villa America. Gerald died in 1964, and Sara died eleven years later.

Acknowledgments

I would like to thank my longtime editor, Erin Clarke, and my literary agents, Molly Friedrich and Lucy Carson, for their support of this project and for their considerable patience.

I would also like to extend my gratitude to Laura Donnelly—daughter of Honoria Murphy Donnelly, and granddaughter of Sara and Gerald Murphy—for sharing with me artifacts from the family's life at Villa America, including jewelry, clothing, maps, photos, and other treasured items.

To my husband and daughter: thank you for your patience as well, and for being great sources of inspiration and love as I wrote this book.

About the Author

LESLEY M. M. BLUME is an author, journalist, and historian based in Los Angeles. Her adult nonfiction book *Everybody Behaves Badly: The True Story Behind Hemingway's Masterpiece "The Sun Also Rises"* was a *New York Times* bestseller, documents the lives of Hemingway, the Fitzgeralds, and the Murphys in France in the 1920s. *Alice Atherton's Grand Tour* is her seventh book for young readers.